MUST THEY DIE?

*The Strange Case of the Prairie Dog
and the Black-Footed Ferret*

THE STRANGE CASE OF THE PRAIRIE DOG
AND THE BLACK-FOOTED FERRET

Must They Die?

by Faith McNulty

Doubleday & Company, Inc., Garden City, New York
1971

The contents of this book appeared originally in
The New Yorker © 1970, in slightly different form.

Foreword

S. Dillon Ripley, Secretary of the Smithsonian Institution, believes that in twenty-five years almost all wild animals— perhaps three-quarters of the species living today—will be extinct. Thus, two or three generations from now there will be few people who have seen a living creature in the wild.

Will these future people find this as inexpressibly sad as we do, contemplating it now? Can one miss what one has never had? By definition, one cannot. And yet a person robbed of his inheritance is the poorer whether he knows it or not. The death of the animals will be the end of a long and intimate association. If one consults Genesis, one finds that man's relationship with the animals began shortly after the fifth day, when God gave him dominion over every living thing. (A footnote can soon be added stating that by the year 2000 man had killed most of them.) Or, if one consults the scientists, one is told that in early times the progenitors of men were indistinguishable from the rest of the animal kingdom, becoming altered and estranged only seven or eight million years ago. Even after that, the relationship remained close. Besides hunting animals and eating them, as is normal for a predator, people lived closely with animals, deriving from them material for art, poetry, folklore, fable, philosophy, science, and much of the imagery of their language.

It is difficult to say how the people born fifty or sixty

years from now into a world that is barren of almost any life except that which human beings husband or control will feel about it. Quite likely they will adapt adequately, but they may find some of the past meaningless and puzzling. What, for instance, can it mean to such a person of the future to read of the lion lying down with the lamb, or the way of the serpent upon the rock, the tiger burning bright, the sly fox, the prudent ant, the wolf at the door, or the Owl and the Pussycat going to sea? Will this future reader, leafing through an old book, experience a strange, intuitive twinge of longing as he wonders what it means to be "happy as a lark"?

MUST THEY DIE?

*The Strange Case of the Prairie Dog
and the Black-Footed Ferret*

Bill Pullins is a tough, old, red-faced outdoorsman who works for the United States Bureau of Sport Fisheries and Wildlife in southern South Dakota. He lives in White River, a town with few paved streets, and drives out into the countryside to do his work.

Pullins' district is made up of rolling green plains covered with buffalo grass and marked here and there by soft hills and wooded bottomlands. It is beautiful country—still wide and open. The population is made up of Sioux Indians and of white ranchers who have bought or leased Indian land to raise cattle and a few sheep. The wild-animal life is varied. There are coyotes, foxes, skunks, badgers, bobcats, raccoons, many birds, and a number of rodents. There are still a few survivors of what was once a vast population of the fat brown burrowing ground squirrels called prairie dogs.

Dealing with all this fauna is Pullins' job. During his boyhood, on a ranch, he became a skillful hunter and trapper. After working for a time as a cowboy and a ranch hand, he found that there was a demand for his knowledge of the habits and manners of wild animals, and for thirty years he has worked for the federal government. In the early days, he was called a trapper. Later, his job was dignified with the title of Mammal-Control Agent, and recently the title was changed to District Field Assistant. Whatever it has been called, the job has remained the same—to destroy, by poison, trap, or gun, wild animals whose presence is an economic burden or an annoyance to the landowners in his district.

On the afternoon of August 7, 1964, Pullins paid a professional call on a rancher named Earl Adrian, who runs cattle on ten thousand acres a few miles south of White River. Adrian wanted Pullins to get rid of some prairie dogs.

Prairie dogs live on open grassland, where they dig burrows, each surrounded by a carefully constructed mound of bare earth. They are communal animals, and they dig their burrows within chirping distance of each other, to form what is called a prairie-dog town. Under certain conditions, these towns may spread out to cover hundreds of acres. The prairie dogs feed on succulent grasses around their burrows. The extent to which they rob cattle of forage has never been determined, but grass is usually cropped short where there are prairie-dog towns, and ever since cattlemen came to the plains it has been axiomatic that prairie dogs are a nuisance and should be exterminated.

Pullins had poisoned Adrian's dog town some years previously, but the population had recovered, and now it spread over about three hundred acres. When Pullins got to the ranch, Adrian's son, Dick, took him out to look over the town. The two stood on a small rise while Pullins tried to estimate the size of the poisoning job. Here and there, the plump, short-legged little beasts sat erect on their haunches atop their small earthen battlements, while others foraged in the grass.

Suddenly, Pullins saw something else—an animal that he had sighted no more than a dozen times in his life. The animal sat up, staring at him; it had a long, supple, minklike body and a small, round head. "From a distance, it looked straight and thin, like a short stake stuck in the ground," Pullins said later.

As the men drew closer, the creature seemed more curious than afraid. It had light-brown fur contrasting with black paws, and across its face was a striking black mask, like that of a raccoon. It stared out of large, round shoe-button eyes, and then suddenly took off, in quick, gracefully undulating bounds, and disappeared down a prairie-dog hole. Pullins told Dick Adrian that the animal was a black-footed ferret. These ferrets, he said, lived in prairie-dog towns, and they were very scarce. For the past ten years or so, the National Park Service had been trying to capture some to stock suitable parks, and hadn't had any luck. In fact, some people thought the ferret was nearly extinct. Dick Adrian, a young man who was interested in wildlife, was quite thrilled to learn that the ranch harbored such a rare creature.

As soon as he could, Pullins got word to Walter H. Kittams, a biologist employed by the National Park Service in Omaha, Nebraska, who had long searched for ferrets himself, and who had asked Pullins and other trappers in ferret territory to let him know if they sighted one. Kittams thanked Pullins warmly and asked him to hold off poisoning the dog town. He couldn't come to South Dakota himself, he said, but he would send someone to investigate the ferret. Then Kittams phoned a ranger named Bob Powell, who was in charge of wildlife management at the Badlands National Monument, some seventy-five miles northwest of White River.

A day or two later, Powell drove to Adrian's ranch, stationed himself on the dog town, and spent the day scanning the rolling sea of short grass with binoculars, watching the comings and goings of the prairie dogs and searching, in vain, for the small, slim silhouette of the ferret. Although ferrets do appear in daylight, Powell suspected that they might be more active at night, so after dark he cruised over the dog town in a pickup truck, hoping to catch the gleam of the ferret's eyes in the beam of a searchlight.

The first day and night were fruitless, and so were the second. Powell grew weary, discouraged, and annoyed. He wondered if Pullins had really seen a ferret; if he had, perhaps it had been a transient, and was now long gone. He spent a third night, and still no ferret appeared. In the morning, just as he was collecting his gear to leave, Powell looked up and saw what was unmistakably a ferret sitting up and staring at him from a prairie-dog hole a couple of hundred feet away. Powell picked up his camera and quickly photographed the ferret. Then the animal disappeared. Highly pleased, Powell drove off with his prize.

Kittams had also phoned a friend of his, a biologist named F. Robert Henderson, who worked for the South Dakota Department of Game, Fish, and Parks. He had talked with Henderson in the past about the importance of finding ferrets before they vanished entirely, and Henderson had shown great interest. When Henderson heard about Pullins' sighting, he was excited, and he promised to follow it up. He enlisted a photographer named Glen Titus, and they, too, went in search of the ferret. It failed to appear, but on a tip from a ranch hand they spotted a mother ferret with four young on a dog town three miles to the north, also on Adrian's ranch, and succeeded in filming the whole family.

"The existence of the black-footed ferret was now official," Henderson has since said. "I hoped this would stir up the Bureau in Washington to do something to protect the species. As for me, I was greatly excited. I knew I had seen one of the rarest and most mysterious little mammals in the world—one that had hardly been studied at all. I decided I'd study it myself—on my own time, if necessary. I was all fired up to help save the ferret. I had no idea what a heartbreaker that was going to be."

II

Pullins' discovery of the ferret occurred during a particularly eventful period in wildlife affairs, and at a particularly embarrassing moment for his employers, the Bureau of Sport Fisheries and Wildlife. That year, a project to protect wildlife in danger of extinction was coming to fruition, and in early July 1964—a month before Pullins spotted the ferret—Stewart L. Udall, the Secretary of the Interior, had announced that the Bureau was compiling a list of "rare or endangered" animals. *Mustela nigripes*, the black-footed ferret, stood out as one of the species that were in most imminent peril. Thus, the welfare of the ferrets on the Adrian ranch, and of whatever relatives they might have, became an official responsibility of the Bureau.

Unofficially, it became a small but persistent headache. The headache arose from the fact that it was the Bureau itself—with its force of agents like Pullins—that had brought the species to the brink of extinction. This had come about because of a peculiarity of the ferret's way of life. *Mustela nigripes* lives almost exclusively among prairie dogs, depending on them for food and shelter. It is logical to assume that where the prairie dog is destroyed so is the ferret. The Bureau had never purposely poisoned ferrets, but it had conducted campaigns against prairie dogs for many years, and the ferret's numbers had dwindled along with the prairie dogs. The Bureau's plans to poison prairie dogs on thousands

7

of acres of South Dakota—the home of the only known remaining ferrets—could quite easily be the coup de grâce.

The Bureau's peculiar duality in its policy on wildlife, which seeks on the one hand to conserve and on the other to destroy large segments of our animal population, is of long standing. It is one of the ironies of this country's system of dealing with wildlife that the agency charged with protecting it is also directed by Congress to destroy "predators and rodents," and does so on a vast scale. Since the lives of all animals are interrelated, and since a great many of our native species are either predators or rodents, it is obvious that to kill predators and rodents while preserving "wildlife" is an impossible trick. The conflict of purposes has always been apparent, but the case of the ferret put it tidily in a nutshell. In fact, *Mustela nigripes* has brought on a crisis in what was already a bad case of governmental schizophrenia.

Like most such cases, this one was a long time developing, but it has become acute as a result of the relatively new concept that animals have a value aside from what can be computed in dollars. This idea, of course, is directly contrary to the notion that tangible value is all that matters, and the accompanying belief that anything that costs anyone money—a coyote that eats a sheep, for instance, or a prairie dog that takes up space on the range—must be destroyed. Conservationists, who beg for recognition of the intangible value—scientific, ecological, and aesthetic—of wild fauna, are continually coming up against practices and ideas evolved solely from the economics of the past.

In earlier times, when almost all wild animals had little or no monetary value, they belonged to no one. Anyone had a right to kill anything he pleased, subject only to the

8

laws of trespass. Fur and game animals were hunted and trapped. Almost all other species large enough to be noticed were considered "varmints," and it was a rural duty and a pleasure to kill them. As game animals grew scarce, the states enacted laws to protect them. Such laws imply that the public has a right to these animals that supersedes the right of the owner of the land on which the animals live. All the states now claim the right to "manage" their fauna. In almost all cases, however, management is still related to economic value. When state conservation departments speak of promoting "wildlife," they actually mean only those species prized by hunters. Game birds and game animals are a billion-dollar business, and the states zealously protect them in order to harvest hunters' votes and dollars. Predators and "nuisance" animals—foxes, skunks, raccoons, and so on—are methodically destroyed, by state wardens, and through bounties paid to hunters, and by arrangement with the Bureau of Sport Fisheries and Wildlife. The rest of the fauna is more or less ignored.

The federal government's role in deciding the fate of the nation's wildlife is considerably less clear-cut than the states'. The Department of the Interior has responsibility for many basic resources, and wildlife is considered a resource. However, only in protecting migratory birds and in dealing with animals on certain public lands does the Department exercise its authority absolutely. Elsewhere, it must work subject to the rights of the states and the rights of private property. Even on the vast public lands of the West, which cover almost a third of the United States, there are conflicting claims to authority over wildlife, and its management is in the hands of separate agencies. The United States Forest Service, an agency of the Department of Agriculture, controls 186,500,000 acres, which are managed in part to produce timber and other crops. When wildlife—rodents, for instance—interferes, it is often eliminated. The Bureau of Land Management, within the Department of the Interior, controls 475,000,000 acres—an area more than three times the size of Texas. This land is open to what Congress has called "multiple use"—sheep and cattle grazing, mining, logging, and so on. Wherever native wildlife conflicts with any of these uses, it has traditionally received rather low consideration.

The agency through which the Department of the Interior manages wildlife is the Fish and Wildlife Service, which consists of the Bureau of Commercial Fisheries and the Bureau of Sport Fisheries and Wildlife. The latter produces hatchery fish for stocking, regulates the hunting of migratory birds, does research, primarily on fish and waterfowl, and operates a system of wildlife refuges—most of them open to hunting—which, though they occupy twenty-eight million acres, are only a small fraction of the acreage controlled by the Forest Service and the Bureau of Land Management. In addition, the Bureau of Sport Fisheries and Wildlife contains a large and powerful division whose primary function is the killing of mountain lions, wolves, coyotes, bobcats, foxes, skunks, bears, porcupines, badgers, various birds, and a number of other species held to be injurious to agriculture, forestry, livestock, or the general welfare.

On public land, the Bureau does this work by arrangement with the Forest Service, the Bureau of Land Management, or whatever other agency controls the land. On private land or state land, it works through arrangements with state conservation departments or with landowners. It functions very much like a commercial exterminating firm, performing its services wherever a contract has been let. East of the Mississippi, this work is relatively small-scale, but in the western states the Bureau employs a field force that in peak seasons reaches a thousand men, who annually poison more than a million acres to destroy rodents, and shoot, trap, and poison possibly several hundred thousand larger wild animals.

There is no accurate measure of how many animals the Bureau kills, but the total might be indicated by a tally of its primary lethal devices. Over the last ten years, it has distributed 6,400,000 strychnine baits, staked out 140,000 chunks of poisoned meat, each large enough to last a season, and logged 410,000 "getter years." (A "getter," designed primarily to kill coyotes, is a cyanide device with a scented wick. It is stuck in the ground, and it injects cyanide into the mouth of any animal that tugs at the wick. Periodically, fired getters are replaced. The Bureau tallies by counting locations where these devices have been in use for a year, rather than by counting the times the getter is replaced.) The Bureau's laboratory, at Denver, is primarily busy with developing and testing new poisons and lethal devices.

The purpose of this vast destruction is, of course, to aid husbandry. It is a form of subsidy for farmers, cattlemen, and sheepmen, relieving them of that part of their overhead which would otherwise be spent on protecting their flocks and fields from marauding animals. Advocates of the system say that land yields a larger crop when it is free of competing wildlife, and that removing the wildlife is no more than sound "management practice." Biologists and conservationists argue, however, that the matter is a lot more complicated than that, both ecologically and philosophically.

They admit that under certain circumstances eradicating

wild animals does indeed save someone money, but they point out that the fauna eradicated is also of value to society. They raise the question of whose interest is greater—that of the individual profiting from the land or that of society, whose interest in the land is not confined to a particular use at a particular time. They object with especial vehemence when wildlife is destroyed on public lands, at public expense, for the short-term profit of individuals who lease it from the public and who are, many of them feel, already overexploiting it. And they say that widespread poisoning may have ecological consequences that will prove impossible to reverse.

Those in favor of "control"—as animal killing is called in the trade—retort that if society wants wild animals on any land, public or private, someone must pay the cost of supporting them. This, of course, is something for which no provision has been made. Ironically, the Bureau generally takes only an advisory role in the extermination of the one animal that is unanimously regarded as undesirable—the urban rat—on the grounds that rat killing by the government would offer unfair competition to private industry.

The existence of the animal-killing division within the Bureau of Sport Fisheries and Wildlife is something of a historical accident. Around the turn of the century, what little concern the government had with wildlife was centered in the now defunct Biological Survey, an agency of the Department of Agriculture. In the years when the West was being opened, settlers encountered a virtually unknown world of plants and animals. The Department of Agriculture undertook scientific studies to help farmers and cattlemen make the best use of the land, and the Biological Survey offered primarily an advisory service. Among other things, it published bulletins on such subjects as how to trap wolves and how to poison prairie dogs, but it left the work up to the interested parties.

In the western states, the sheepmen, the cattlemen, and the farmers were doing a pretty thorough job, sometimes on their own, sometimes with state money and manpower, of thinning out the enormous numbers of animals—wolves, mountain lions, bears, bobcats, and coyotes—that menaced livestock, and also of keeping down the population of prairie dogs, which flourished wherever the buffalo had ranged. Until the First World War, varmint extermination received no direct federal help. Then, with the sudden demand to increase beef production to feed the Army, western congressmen asked for federal money and manpower.

Congress appropriated $125,000 for the Biological Survey, which used the money to hire hunters to kill wolves. Sheepmen soon demanded and got a program to kill coyotes. Thus, quite suddenly, the Biological Survey was transformed from an advisory agency into an active one. Its services were popular in the West, and its officials discovered that, whereas Congress had been stingy with money for research, it was remarkably generous with money for killing predators and rodents.

The newborn service, later named Predator and Rodent Control, or PARC, soon took on all the aspects of a well-nourished bureaucracy. Administrators in Washington mapped the West into districts, and supervisors directed a force of field men who trapped, shot, and poisoned coyotes, bobcats, and mountain lions—and, incidentally, much of the other fauna—wherever they found them. Cattlemen and sheepmen, who until then had relied on hired hands to protect their property, were delighted to have the animal killing done for them, and praised the congressmen who had arranged this convenient subsidy for them. The PARC men, anxious for more appropriations, issued streams of bulletins and assorted propaganda describing the ravages of predators and rodents.

The result was a huge increase in the killing of wild animals. Whereas the average landowner had gone to the expense of killing animals only in his immediate vicinity, the PARC men zealously expanded their work to remote regions. Since a trap or a bit of poisoned meat may kill a variety of animals other than the intended victim, the program amounted to a generalized war on the wildlife of the West. As the work of trapping and poisoning expanded during the 1920's scientists outside the government became increasingly alarmed and incensed. Conservationists began to protest.

In 1930, a million-dollar appropriation for killing predators and rodents was pending in Congress. That year, the American Society of Mammalogists held a symposium at the American Museum of Natural History in New York, and those present bitterly attacked the poisoning program and begged the Biological Survey to conduct scientific studies before plunging ahead with further extermination. Dr. Charles C. Adams, director of the New York State Museum, read a statement saying, "As field naturalists of many years experience . . . we strongly protest the excessive expenditure of public funds for drastic reduction of predatory animals in advance of satisfactory proof of the soundness of that policy. Elimination of these animals is almost certain to be followed by excessive increase of mice, rabbits and other rodents . . . This will necessitate continual appropriations for the government poison squad. We urge provision for comprehensive scientific study *first*, as the only basis for intelligent control."

Other speakers pointed to the disaster of the Kaibab Forest, a classic case in the annals of mismanagement. Between 1907 and 1923 on the Kaibab plateau, north of the Grand Canyon, government hunters waged war on the mountain lions for the supposed benefit of the deer herds. The result was sadly opposite. The deer multiplied and overgrazed to such an extent that they turned the area into a wasteland. As a result thousands of deer died of starvation and the area may never recover its former verdancy. The officials of PARC shrugged off this unfortunate episode and seemed impatient with talk of ecology. One of them remarked, "When Congress gives the Biological Survey orders to do a certain thing they are going to do it," implying that the will of the people absolved PARC of any ecological responsibility.

After the symposium, events took an unexpected twist. Congress held up not only the appropriation for killing predators but *all* funds for the Biological Survey. Officials of the Survey pleaded with the American Society of Mammalogists to relax its opposition, in order not to destroy the entire Survey, with its wildlife refuges and research programs. In return, they promised to reduce their killing program and to refine their methods to minimize needless destruction of animal life. The mammalogists relented to the extent of sending Congress a message saying that their criticisms applied only to predator control, and the appropriation was restored. The chief of PARC was replaced, the work force was reduced, and a new start was made. To the indignation of the mammalogists who are veterans of this skirmish, officials of the Survey and its successor

Bureau misrepresented the message that saved them as constituting approval of predator control by the American Society of Mammalogists.

Among other things this episode made clear was that PARC's activities rested on rather shaky legal grounds, since they derived entirely from a fifteen-year-old congressional directive to kill wolves. Those in favor of control hastened to shore up PARC's position. In 1931, Congress passed an act directing the Secretary of Agriculture to conduct campaigns for the destruction of mountain lions, wolves, coyotes, bobcats, prairie dogs, gophers, ground squirrels, jackrabbits, and other animals that were "injurious" to agriculture, horticulture, forestry, husbandry, game, or domestic animals, or that carried disease. Thus, any wild animal that might be considered injurious by practically anyone for any reason was on the official death list. The only limit to the execution of the act was money. Funds to carry it out would have to be appropriated anew each year.

In 1940, the Biological Survey was transferred from the Department of Agriculture to the Department of the Interior and was renamed the United States Fish and Wildlife Service. PARC eventually became part of the Service's Bureau of Sport Fisheries and Wildlife. Despite the new leaf turned over in 1930, PARC activities again crept upward. From 1940 to 1950, the money spent for predator control nearly doubled, rising from $2,714,023 to $4,629,053, but this was perhaps not a true measure of PARC's increased effectiveness in killing animals, for in 1944 a new poison, sodium fluoroacetate, known as 1080, was first used by the Fish and Wildlife Service.

This poison is fantastically lethal. From the point of view of those wishing to increase the number of animals

16

that could be killed at small expense, the introduction of 1080 marked a tremendous advance. From the point of view of conservationists, it was a disaster.

Sodium fluoroacetate was first made in the laboratory nearly a hundred years ago, but its extraordinary potentialities were not recognized until the Second World War, when two Polish scientists, fleeing the war, brought the compound to England. During the war, the United States was cut off from foreign suppliers of poison, and the Office of Scientific Research and Development underwrote a search for new poisons with which to combat plague carried by rats in war-ravaged areas. At the same time, the research branch of the Bureau of Sport Fisheries and Wildlife was looking for a new poison to use against coyotes as well as rodents; it wanted one that would be cheaper and more effective than its staple poisons, strychnine and thallium sulphate, both of which had serious disadvantages. It undertook to test new poisons for the Office of Research and Development. On June 8, 1944, sodium fluoroacetate, which had the invoice number 1080, was tested at the Bureau's laboratory in Denver. It proved extraordinarily deadly. Research was hastened, and within a year 1080 was in use.

Sodium fluoroacetate is a white salt that looks like powdered sugar and is odorless and tasteless. It dissolves in water, and it is slow to deteriorate—two qualities that make it ideal for use in poison bait. To kill predators, a water solution of 1080 is injected with a syringe into a fifty- or hundred-pound piece of meat, which is staked out. This lethal chunk of meat, known as a bait station, will last an entire season. To kill rodents, grain is soaked in a 1080 solution and then scattered. The poison acts on the animal's central nervous system, producing violent convulsions and vomiting, followed by death.

Whether it is a less painful death than that brought on by other poisons has naturally not been determined, but the Bureau frequently refers to 1080 as "humane."

After an animal swallows a dose of 1080, there is a period of thirty minutes or more with no effects, and the animal may not die for two hours. This delay means that 1080 victims frequently die at some distance from the bait (dead coyotes have been found four miles from the site of the poison), so an accurate count of fatalities is impossible.

Sodium fluoroacetate is remarkably cheap, $15 a pound, and tiny amounts are effective. Sixteen grams, worth twenty-eight cents, will poison a thousand pounds of horsemeat sufficiently to kill a coyote that eats only 1.4 ounces of the bait. Ground squirrels are killed by eating one grain of seed bait prepared at the rate of one pound of 1080 to two tons of grain, so that $15 worth of 1080 could kill 1,800,000 ground squirrels. This economy is a shining advantage in the eyes of its users, and yet another factor frightening to conservationists.

The most disastrous property of 1080, however, is its stability. It does not break down in the body of its victim, and this means that any animal or bird that feeds on the carcass of a 1080 victim may be poisoned, and its body may become another lethal bait. Furthermore, the dying animals vomit deadly doses of undigested meat, attractive to many animals and birds, wherever they go. Almost all carnivorous birds and small carnivorous mammals will eat carrion, so the possibilities of this chain reaction are extensive.

Even Bureau biologists acknowledge that this is a "weakness" of 1080, but they maintain that conservationists exaggerate it. Advocates of 1080 point instead to the fact that different species differ in their susceptibility to the poison.

Canines are particularly susceptible. In general, birds are more resistant to 1080 than mammals. Critics of 1080 say that these variations in tolerance are a distinction without a difference, because all our native meat-eating animals and birds are capable of eating enough coyote bait to kill them. Eagles have been killed by 1080 put out for coyotes, and California condors, which conservationists are trying desperately to save, have died from eating ground squirrels poisoned by 1080.

Human beings are a happy exception to the general rule of susceptibility to 1080 as it is used in coyote bait. A man would have to eat more than eight pounds of meat poisoned for coyotes in order to be killed. There have been two episodes in which thieves stole and ate chunks of poisoned horsemeat and survived. When 1080 is dissolved in water, however, it is a different matter. One teaspoonful of the solution used to kill rats could kill a child, and three teaspoons could kill an adult. There is no antidote to a dose of 1080. There have been thirteen accidental deaths of humans, five deaths possibly due to 1080, and six non-fatal poisonings. This, however, is probably a better record than that of thallium and strychnine, the poisons that 1080 has now largely replaced.

An example of what 1080 can do was provided in British Columbia. Until 1949 the wolf population there was high. Sheepmen and cattlemen were protesting their losses, the government was finding bounty payments too expensive. Conservation Department officials, who had found the old-fashioned methods of poisoning with strychnine and cyanide comparatively ineffective over large areas of wilderness, began using 1080 in 1950. In a massive assault on the wolves, the Canadian Predator Control Division poisoned an area of 200,-000 square miles with 2,100 baits treated with 1080, each large enough to kill hundreds of wolves. Eighty per cent of the 1080 baits were dropped from airplanes, so that even road-less areas were reached. Wolves and coyotes became "conspic-uous by their absence," the Conservation Department reported later. Wolf bounty payments dropped to almost nothing. The operation was repeated a second year, and thereafter so few wolves were left that bounties were removed and bait-ing was cut in half. No one counted the incidental victims. The Supervisor for Predator Control in British Columbia said, "It has been possible to control the larger wild canines almost at will. . . ." This is exactly what ecologists, fearful of the final effects on wildlife of killing off all predators (which have an important role in the well-being of prey species), and conservationists, who mourn the passing of wolves from their last refuge, find so alarming about 1080.

The whole matter of the export of 1080 to other countries where there may be even fewer limitations on its use than exist here is yet another facet of the horror that conservation-ists see in the poison. The Bureau cooperates with poison campaigns in Mexico, and in 1963, 1080 provided by the Bureau killed grizzly bears surviving as a small remnant in the remote Sierra del Nido. In 1969 the Journal of the British Preservation Society reported the bears extinct. South Africa, which has many troublesome animals, heard about the control techniques so successfully developed in America. Its Bureau of Nature Conservation asked for help in initiating a poison-ing program. The Bureau of Sport Fisheries and Wildlife dis-patched one of its experts, who showed the South Africans how to destroy baboons, black-backed jackals, gophers, and a number of other species. The rest is up to the Department of Nature Conservation. Obviously there are few countries so poor and backward that they cannot afford some 1080 and a few airplanes to scatter it wherever they wish, and there are few undeveloped countries where the residents do not find one or more species of wild animals a pest on one or another occasion. Thus, it is now possible for whole ecosystems of animals and birds to be extirpated from vast areas at the whim of government or of land exploiters who happen to think it would be a good idea. There was no exaggeration in a statement by Eric A. Peacock, a Bureau biologist, who wrote that 1080 has "the potential of a biological high explosive."

At about the time 1080 came into general use, the profits of the sheep industry began to decline, for a variety of reasons. Pinched by higher labor costs, the sheepmen began to run larger flocks with fewer herdsmen, and the flocks became more vulnerable to attack by coyotes. During the fifties, the sheepmen began an aggressive campaign for more coyote killing by the Bureau, and in 1956 the House Appropriations Committee held hearings on the sheepmen's demands. Sixteen United States representatives from western states showed up to describe the fearful losses that coyotes were causing the sheepmen. At a similar Senate hearing, western senators chided the Bureau for neglecting its responsibility for killing coyotes.

Eventually, the chairman of the Senate Appropriations Committee, Senator Carl Hayden, of Arizona, asked the director of the Fish and Wildlife Service, "How much money could you really use? According to the livestock industry . . . you are not keeping up with the predators." The director, faced by an embarrassment of riches, replied, "I do not think I am able to answer that too well. . . . I would be glad to have our section on that work prepare a statement for you, sir."

The challenge of how to spend more money was one that PARC proved well able to meet. It submitted a statement that began, "The Fish and Wildlife Service can very effectively use an increase of a million dollars for the control of predatory animals and injurious rodents." The Senate Appropriations Committee thereupon increased the Service's funds for that purpose from $969,500 to $1,759,000. Funds of state and local origin raised the total to $4,558,416. Thus, a working arrangement was established between PARC and the sheepmen's lobby. The noted wildlife biologist Durward Allen, a critic of PARC, said at an annual meeting of the National Audubon Society, "The predator-control program . . . has . . . its own pipeline around the Bureau of the Budget directly to the Appropriations Committees of Congress." After this transfusion of money, PARC bloomed. By 1961, it was employing six hundred and seventy-five field men, and last year there were around eight hundred. In 1969, the Bureau spent slightly more than seven million dollars killing wildlife.

At the hearings in 1956, no voice was raised in protest against increased funds for control, probably because only the partisans of the program knew what was going on, but conservationists soon became aware and raised their voices loudly. Dr. E. Raymond Hall, who had been one of the scientists to assail the program back in 1931, again rose to the attack. He had become one of the most distinguished mammalogists in the country, and was, among other things, chairman of the Zoology Department of the University of Kansas, director of its museum, and state zoologist of Kansas. He was also vice-president of an organization called Defenders of Wildlife, which has more than twenty thousand members and publishes a quarterly nature magazine called *Defenders of Wildlife News*, which, much to the annoyance of the predator controllers in the Bureau, attacked their activities in almost every issue.

Defenders of Wildlife, joined by the National Audubon Society, rallied conservationists, both lay and professional, who made their opinions felt in Congress. In 1963, Representative John D. Dingell, of Michigan, offered a bill to strip PARC of much of its money and its manpower and restrict its activities to an advisory service on animal-damage problems. This threat, together with growing remonstrances by qualified scientists, caused Secretary Udall to appoint an advisory board to look into the whole matter of wild-animal killing. The chairman of the advisory board was Dr. A. Starker Leopold, professor of wildlife management at the University of California, and the four other members were well known in wildlife circles. There were Dr. Ira N. Gabrielson, president of the Wildlife Management Institute, and Dr. Clarence Cottam, director of the Welder Wildlife Foundation, who had been director and assistant director of the Fish and Wildlife Service some years before. There were also Thomas L. Kimball, executive director of the National Wildlife Federation, and Dr. Stanley A. Cain, professor of conservation at the University of Michigan's School of Natural Resources; Dr. Cain later became Assistant Secretary of the Interior for Fish and Wildlife and Parks.

The Leopold Board, as it was called, proceeded from two basic tenets: first, that all native animals are resources of value to the people of the United States, and, second, that "local population control" is essential where a species causes "significant" damage. It then attempted to estimate the total amount of animal destruction carried out in the name of protecting property.

In the West, the Bureau is not the sole executioner of wildlife. Many predators, rodents, and "nuisance animals" are killed under programs administered by state departments of agriculture, public health, and fish and game, and by county agents and livestock associations. Sometimes they combine their activities, and these combined activities, the Board's report said, "are complicated almost beyond belief." The Board therefore found it impossible to ascertain the real extent of poisoning, trapping, and shooting, or the annual toll of wildlife. The Bureau bears the central responsibility, however, since it does by far the major share of the work.

A factor that complicates this responsibility, the Board found, is the peculiar way in which PARC is financed. In addition to the money provided by Congress, it receives funds from its customers, who may be other federal bureaus, state and county agencies, or livestock associations. PARC gets these by negotiating contracts, or "cooperative agreements," whereby it provides the service but more than half of the cost is shared by those "benefitting" from its work. This outside financing enormously expands the work that PARC can do, but it also gives agencies or groups that have paid for control a voice in determining where, when, and how much animal killing is done. This system, the Board reported, puts the fate of wildlife in the hands of its enemies and excludes its friends.

The Leopold Board went on to investigate the workings of PARC, and its report revealed a situation every bit as ghastly as the conservationists had said it was. PARC men, from supervisors to trappers, had gone about the West pressing their services as though they were peddling vacuum cleaners. Killing was their business, and dead animals were their product. PARC men searched out situations in which animals might conceivably do damage, and then went about rousing rural opinion against the animals and describing the benefits that "control" could bring to farmer, rancher, and hunter. The Leopold Report said of this, "When professional hunters are employed, control tends to become an end in itself and, following Parkinson's Law, the machinery for its accomplishment can easily proliferate beyond real need."

Contributing to PARC's expansion was the frontier philosophy of the West, which took it for granted that killing animals was a good thing and that killing more of them was necessarily better. Within the Bureau itself PARC had become the most powerful branch. With former PARC men in policy positions, any collision between PARC's work and that of other branches was usually settled in favor of PARC. These men were also inclined to look the other way when the Bureau's own rules were violated by the men in the field. The Leopold Board examined the techniques PARC men were supposed to follow, many of which had been designed to minimize the effect of lethal devices on animals other than the intended victims. Poisoned baits, for instance, were supposed to be a certain distance apart, and no more than one to a township, so that small animals with a shorter range than the coyote might still exist unpoisoned in the spaces between the baits. Baits were supposed to be picked up in the spring, when hibernating animals appear. In the interests of either convenience or efficiency in killing, however, the rules were often ignored, with the result that even more wildlife than intended was being killed.

One question to which the Board addressed itself was the criteria by which PARC determined that killing of wildlife was economically justified in any given situation. Logically, the Committee noted, a decision should be related to some objective measure, such as the value of property being protected. In fact, the Board found, very little objective data existed, and when facts did exist they seemed to play a small role in decisions. In each local situation the PARC man concerned made his own judgment of the wisdom of undertaking a killing program. Some supervisors were reluctant to kill animals needlessly, but others went along willingly with any proposal from livestock owners or local agricultural interests. Thus, animals were killed wherever anyone wanted them killed and money was made available. PARC's primary interest, the Board said, was to "build programs" and keep its men busy. As a result, coyotes, whose only sin is that they sometimes kill sheep, were poisoned in areas where there were no sheep; porcupines, which gnaw timber, were destroyed where there were no valuable trees, and so on through a long list of tragic absurdities. A great deal of PARC's killing, the Board found, rested on the most tenuous rationalizations or none at all.

While the Board conceded that economic gain does accrue from killing animals, it felt that the question of just when such gain outweighs the cost of killing, both in money and in ecological loss, is extremely difficult to determine. Between the two extremes—senseless killing, on the one hand, and, on the other, the advantage to a sheep owner of clearing a lambing ground of coyotes—lies a vast area in which much depends upon the point of view. A poultryman with a few hundred dollars' worth of turkeys might prefer to have all possible marauders killed, while a conservationist might deem the money better spent on building a predator-proof pen.

Cost figures are elusive. No one has attempted to weigh the value of wildlife in money. Even the cost of killing is hard to determine in any particular instance, since most of the cost is "overhead." Equally unknown, the Leopold Board discovered, was the cost of damage that animals cause. Except in a few local situations, no objective agency had ever gathered valid statistics. What few figures PARC had collected came from unverified reports by the livestock owners themselves. Sheepmen, fearful of having PARC's services withdrawn, regularly exaggerate the extent of coyote damage; any sheep, dead for any reason (and sheep are prone to sudden demise for countless reasons), are usually charged to coyotes. Ranchers may ascribe their troubles to prairie dogs rather than to overgrazing. And there are numerous other variables, such as herding and husbandry practices, that blur the statistical picture. The Board found that PARC, lacking any real data, was using a series of guesses and unverified estimates of damage to justify its seven-million-dollar investment to kill animals.

The Board also questioned some of the biological assumptions on which PARC based its case against assorted wildlife. There is, for instance, the question of whether or not coyotes kill calves. PARC stoutly maintained that they do, and that it was thus justified in killing coyotes to aid cattle ranchers. Some cattlemen agree, but others deny it, and some have even protested coyote killing on the range, on the ground that coyotes keep down the rodent population. The Leopold Board concluded that calf killing by coyotes was so rare that it justified killing coyotes only in a locality where their depredations against calves could be irrefutably proved.

Bobcats, the Board found, were on PARC's death list as predators on poultry, on game birds, and even on calves and lambs. The Board deplored the widespread killing of bobcats, finding that the damage they do is usually negligible. In areas where there were no domestic animals to be protected, PARC nevertheless killed predators, ostensibly to protect other wildlife. Except in rare situations, the Board said, native birds and mammals need no such protection.

In presenting its case to the public or to Congress or the Bureau of the Budget, PARC usually stresses its mission "to protect human health and safety." Few people are inclined to question such a laudable goal or to ask just how the Bureau accomplishes it. In fact opportunities to do so are rare. The mountain lion and the grizzly bear are not widespread menaces.

There is, however, the problem of rabies, and PARC has relied heavily on its anti-rabies campaigns to win popular approval. Rabies is endemic among coyotes, foxes, raccoons, skunks, and bats, and usually goes unnoticed. When rabies comes to public attention, as when there is an increase of cases or when a human being or a domestic animal is exposed, there is consternation. The public demands "action." Unfortunately, science has not yet determined what this action should be. The only sure way to wipe out rabies would be totally to exterminate furbearers, which is not, as yet, thought practical. Nevertheless, when rabies appears in the wild, PARC is summoned by local health authorities, and rides to the rescue with baskets of poisoned eggs to destroy the local skunks, coons, foxes, and so on.

In scientific circles, there is considerable doubt as to whether this is the right thing to do. Some epidemiologists suspect that studies may show that poisoning campaigns protract and spread rabies rather than halting it. Left alone, they say, rabies epidemics quickly come to a peak and decline as all the susceptible animals in the area either die or become immune. If poison thins the population, killing the immune as well as the susceptible, there are fewer disease-spreading contacts between animals. With competitors removed, the animals that escape the poison travel more widely. The disease smoulders on and is given more time and opportunity to spread. The Leopold Report said, "A great deal of animal control is pursued on the basis that it is necessary to control rabies, but the facts regarding this situation are scant indeed

. . . scientific proof of the assertion is lacking." However, the Report added, because of the fear rabies inspires it can be expected that outbreaks of rabies will invariably lead to animal-control programs. The Board deplored PARC's tendency to exploit this situation and to lean heavily on rabies control to justify its existence.

In the arid West, upswings in the rodent population can have a serious effect on crops and pastureland. When the land is overgrazed, rodents thrive, and when the land is returned to a healthy condition, they diminish. Killing rodents is merely treating a symptom of land abuse. The Bureau admits this, but calls rodent poisoning "a step toward reclamation." Conservationists observe that there is no guarantee that poisoning will be followed by reclamation and that it may have served only to postpone it.

The Leopold Report conceded that "under existing land use practices some rodent control is essential," but it deplored the use of 1080 to poison rodents. (In 1963, PARC poisoned a million and a quarter acres with two hundred and fifty thousand pounds of bait, of which a hundred and fifty thousand pounds had been soaked in 1080. There is no way of measuring the acreage poisoned by local authorities, but it was probably more.)

The report upheld what the conservationists had been saying all along—that secondary poisoning from eating poisoned rodents can have a "heavy impact" on small carnivores and some birds. It noted that in many regions where there were no sheep and where coyote damage was negligible, the coyote had been "essentially extirpated" as a secondary result of rodent poisoning. In addition, it noted, uncounted numbers of badgers, bears, foxes, raccoons, skunks, opossums, eagles, hawks, owls, and vultures had thus been exposed to 1080.

"The black-footed ferret . . . is nearing extinction, and the primary cause is almost certainly poisoning campaigns among the prairie dogs," the report said, and it went on, "In short, secondary poisoning of unintended victims of 1080 distributed primarily for rodents is, in the opinion of this Board, a major problem in animal control which requires regulation."

The Board recommended that the Secretary of the Interior explore legal means to ban 1080 as a poison for field rodents and to prevent "ecological abuse," as in the case of insecticides. It also deplored the export of 1080 to Mexico or any country "where the danger of misuse is substantial."

What PARC's killing adds up to is, of course, anybody's guess. PARC records the numbers of known dead animals only in certain cases, and it obviously cannot record those whose bodies are not found. It submitted to the Leopold Board a table listing the numbers of animals whose bodies had been recorded over a one-year period, and these figures may be taken as a minimum starting point. It showed 842 bears, 20,780 lynxes and bobcats, 89,653 coyotes, 294 mountain lions, 2,779 wolves (mostly red wolves, which resemble coyotes), 6,941 badgers, 1,170 beavers, 24,273 foxes, 7,615 opossums, 6,685 porcupines, 10,078 raccoons, 19,052 skunks, and 601 "miscellaneous" victims.

The Board made a number of recommendations. First, that wildlife should have a voice in court. The Board found that economic interests had ample expression but that conservationists were unrepresented. It urged the Secretary of the Interior to appoint an advisory board to include conservationists and scientists as well as woolgrowers and cattlemen. The Board also recommended that PARC "completely reassess its function and purpose," and commented, "There persists a traditional point of view that the PARC operation is responsible primarily to livestock and agricultural interests and that the growing interest of the general public in all wild animal life is a potential obstruction . . . to be evaded and circumvented wherever possible." It warned that if PARC continued its policies the conservationists would probably succeed in dismantling the program entirely, and it urged that PARC's goal therefore be an "absolute minimum [of killing] consistent with proven needs to protect other resources. . . ."

Though nobody knows just how much property damage is done by wild animals, everyone will acknowledge that there are some real losses. Devising a system that gives reasonable protection to property and also to wildlife is not an easy matter. The problem is most acute in regard to the sheep rancher. Unfortunately coyotes do indeed kill sheep and poison is the most economical way to deal with them. If federal control were removed, the sheepmen would undoubtedly use poison on their own unless they were somehow prohibited from doing so. In that case they would be forced to employ herders with guns to protect their flocks. From the point of view of wildlife this is the best solution since only the target animal would be killed, but the sheepmen claim the added cost would put them out of business. This arouses no sympathy from conservationists who feel that in any case woolgrowing is a poor use of land, particularly public land. They point out that most of our wool is imported anyway and that sheep-grazing on dry western pastures does far more damage to the land than it returns in profit to the economy. If sheep cannot co-exist with wildlife they feel the sheep rather than the wildlife should be the ones to go.

The Leopold Board avoided the fundamental question of whether sheep should be grown at the expense of wildlife, but it pointed out that in the far West in sheep country, control presented a different problem than it did elsewhere. In this instance, and in this instance only, the Board declared that the PARC system, if properly administered, could do a more efficient and perhaps less damaging job than if control were left to the states and private interests.

The Board defined sheep country as that west of a line drawn from north to south following the 98th meridian and running from the center of North Dakota through eastern Texas. On all the land to the east of this line the Board recommended that PARC discontinue its field work entirely and be replaced by an "extension system" modeled after the system used in Kansas and Missouri. These two states have never bought federal predator control but have handled animal damage problems by employing two or three experts in the state's Department of Agriculture. The animal damage specialists provide information and technical advice to any landowner who asks for it, but leave the work up to the individual. A farmer bothered by raccoons, for instance, may be told how to set traps, but he is urged not to kill anything more than the offending animal. The system is economical since it involves only the salaries of two or three men compared to the hundreds of thousands of dollars spent by PARC in comparable western states. There is little danger of an extension agent becoming overzealous to protect his job. According to George C. Halazon, who is the extension specialist on wildlife management in Kansas, the system satisfies the needs of landowners and results in far less killing. Landowners who might be inclined to have all their varmints killed off if the service was given them are far less inclined to take the trouble to do it themselves, and usually confine themselves to the specific animal giving trouble. "We often find that when a man with an animal problem is told he has to do his own work the problem just melts away," Halazon has said.

The Board noted that the Bureau of Sport Fisheries and Wildlife had done scant research on ways to minimize animal damage, and suggested it study ways to repel animals rather than kill them, and also develop devices that would kill only the offending animal or species instead of broad segments of the fauna.

In its summary, the Board said, "The program of animal control under . . . PARC . . . has become an end in itself and no longer is a balanced component of an overall scheme of wildlife husbandry. . . . Far more animals are being killed than would be required for effective protection of livestock, agricultural crops, wildland resources and human health. This unnecessary destruction is further augmented by state, county and individual endeavor. The federal government . . . should be setting an example in the proper scientific management of all wildlife resources. . . . Instead PARC has developed into a semi-autonomous bureaucracy whose function . . . bears scant relationship to real need and less still to scientific management."

The Leopold Report was given to Secretary Udall in March 1964, and for more than a year hung in limbo until June 1965, when he announced its acceptance as a "general guidepost for Department policy." Meanwhile, the sheepmen, in alarm, had sent large delegations to Washington to exhort their congressmen not to let control be diminished. In his acceptance of the report, Udall reassured them by saying, "We have no intention of abandoning our responsiblity in the control of damage . . . when it is clear that the Department's assistance is needed."

In October 1964, the director of the Bureau of Sport Fisheries and Wildlife left, and was followed a few months later by the chief of PARC. The new director was John Gottschalk, a generally liked and admired biologist specializing in fish, who had been with the Bureau for nineteen years. Gottschalk announced that a new era was at hand—one in which the Bureau would recognize its total responsibility for wildlife and limit killing to instances of "demonstrated need."

As a first step, PARC was renamed Animal Damage Control and was placed within a newly created division that bore the attractive title of Wildlife Services. Along with the former duties of PARC, Wildlife Services was given responsibility for pesticide appraisal and monitoring and for "wildlife enhancement." To enhance wildlife, the division assigns biologists to study situations—on Indian reservations, for instance—where a change in land-use practices might produce a larger crop of such wildlife as deer or game birds.

Lumping animal-damage control and the enhancement of wildlife in a single division enables the Bureau to describe Wildlife Services' work as "the conservation and management of the Nation's wildlife resources for the use and enjoyment of the entire citizenry." However, since a little under ninety per cent of the funds of Wildlife Services are spent on killing and a little over ten per cent on enhancement, conservationists, though they have welcomed the enhancement program, have found this description a trifle unrealistic and have wondered if the move were more in the interests of camouflage than reform.

The man named to direct Wildlife Services was Jack H. Berryman, who has a Master's degree in mammalian ecology from the University of Utah, had previously worked for the Bureau as a specialist in wildlife restoration, had been an associate professor of wildlife resources at Utah State University, and is a past president of the Wildlife Society. Berryman announced that he believed firmly in "control" when it was "properly" applied, and he went to work to "professionalize" control practices, rebuild the shattered morale of the division, end the abuses revealed by the Leopold Board, and re-educate the men in the field to think in terms of killing less rather than more.

As he went about reconciling the irreconcilable—killing enough coyotes to keep sheepmen happy, enough rodents to satisfy lumbermen, and enough of whatever else might be troublesome to keep state officials willing to allocate funds for Bureau contracts, and at the same time not completely destroying the fauna of the West—he found on his right flank the livestock industry, ready to fight any decrease in the protection of their interests, and on his left the conservationists, armed with the damning judgments of the Leopold Board.

As time passed, the Bureau seemed eager to forget just what the Leopold Board had said. Conservationists were hardly reassured when Director Gottschalk told a National Wool Growers Association Convention in Portland, Oregon, on January 21, 1966, that the Leopold Board "made no drastic recommendations," and that the report was a general guidepost for policy, not a policy "mandate" or a "working manual for the Bureau."

The conservationists waited for a year after Gottschalk had taken over, but in 1966, when nothing more material than a change of name had become visible to them, returned to the attack. Representative Dingell introduced yet another bill to abolish federal control and replace it with an extension system. Committee hearings were held at which Dr. Stanley A. Cain, now Assistant Secretary of the Interior for Fish and

Wildlife and Parks, testified about the progress of reform. Dr. Cain's position was peculiarly ambivalent, since before his appointment he had been a member of the Leopold Board and had signed the report.

He told the hearing that he believed the Bureau was on the way to a program that could withstand "the scrutiny of all." He believed animal control to be necessary but warned that if it was done improperly it posed a threat to the environment, to wildlife in general, and to human safety. These hazards, he said, made it essential that control be handled only by skilled professionals.

Despite his new confidence in the Bureau, Dr. Cain had difficulty in listing specific reforms. The most substantial change that had been made since PARC was replaced by Animal Damage Control, he said, had been a vigorous effort to re-educate Bureau employees and instill the idea that simply killing as many animals as possible was no longer their goal. Unfortunately, for lack of funds, there had been no new research on actual animal damage, or on wildlife populations, or on the environmental effects of poisoning, all of which the Leopold Board had recommended. No advisory board had been appointed, because it seemed likely that nothing but bloodshed would result from meetings of a board that included both members of Defenders of Wildlife and the woolgrowers. It would, Dr. Cain said, be merely "a forum for hassles." He said that he had hoped to discontinue the use of 1080 but that Mr. Berryman had persuaded him that 1080 was the safest and most effective "tool" they had and that the poisons used before 1080 were worse. He had consulted the Department of Agriculture, which had jurisdiction over the general use of 1080, and had been told that the present regulations governing it were adequate. Thus, nothing had come of the

Leopold Board's recommendation that 1080 be greatly restricted.

The vital questions of defining "a demonstrated need" to kill animals and weighing economic need against the value of wildlife involved, as Gottschalk testified, "a very large gray area." Pending a better solution, Dr. Cain said, the Bureau was handling these questions by asking the users or managers of land who desired control to explain what use of the land was planned, so that the need or lack of need to kill animals would be clearer. Thus, on land identified by the user as lambing ground, coyotes would be killed, while on land identified as recreational they would not. To the conservationists in the audience, this seemed less than a startling breakthrough. It seemed that the Bureau was merely putting the power of decision more firmly than ever in the hands of those who desired, for one reason or another, to have animals eliminated.

At one point, Representative Dingell said to Dr. Cain, "But actually you . . . have nothing to show this committee in terms of concrete changes, with the exception of revision of the internal structure of your agency. . . . Am I correct?"

Dr. Cain replied, "You are not completely correct, I don't believe."

"But I am sort of correct?" Mr. Dingell asked.

Dr. Cain said, "You are essentially correct."

The livestock men and their congressmen also took the stand. Representative O. Clark Fisher, of Texas, representing twenty-three thousand owners of five million sheep and four million angora goats, said that the Bureau should increase its efforts to cope with the "destructive menace" of predation. Not only coyotes and bobcats were on his death list. Killing gray foxes, raccoons, and skunks, he said, would also benefit lamb and kid crops. He did not explain how. The American

Farm Bureau Federation rallied to the side of the sheepmen, saying that predators had no place on public lands when they tended to drive the livestock grazer from the range. "It is easy to be on the side of protecting varmints which inflict loss to someone else's property," a Farm Bureau spokesman said.

Representative E. Y. Berry, of South Dakota, who shares the delusion of many sportsmen that predators determine the abundance of game animals, testified that predators in South Dakota were threatening the hunting industry there. But the chief victim of "senseless destruction" by predators, he said, was the American sheepman. He estimated that sheepmen around the country lost thirty to forty million dollars in a recent year because of predators.

"I do not think that the South Dakota farmers and stockmen are going to stand still for another two or three years while their losses from predators mount," he said. "I do not believe that businessmen, the hotels, the restaurants, the motels, and so forth, who have watched their business dry up because of the lack of decent pheasant hunting, are going to stand still for another two or three more years of 'drought' in the pheasant population. . . . The question is essentially this: Is South Dakota to remain an agricultural state or a wildlife preserve?"

The conservationists also marshalled an impressive array of witnesses, including representatives of Defenders of Wildlife, the National Audubon Society, and America the Beautiful; Dr. E. Raymond Hall, the control system's most tireless foe; other scientists; and variously qualified individuals. They urged the committee to abolish federal predator and rodent controls, their arguments ranging from the ecological to the aesthetic and philosophical. The reckless killing of wildlife, they argued, amounted to depleting a valuable and irreplace-able resource belonging to all the people for the short-term gain of a few.

The most direct and heartfelt speech, however, came not from any of the professionals but from a fur trapper named Paul Maxwell, of Colorado. The policy of the fur trappers, he said, was to take some animals and leave others for seed, but the sheepmen and the Bureau were collaborating on a system capable of destroying everything.

"These control programs . . . are carried on by the sheep ranchers and the federal employees with no compassion, no compunction, qualms, or conscience," he said. "Anything goes. . . . There are no extremes they won't go to in order to get poison, and will break every law of God and man to use it for their selfish, inhuman purposes. . . . As if 1080 poison isn't enough, we have not hundreds but thousands of strychnine pills thrown from airplanes, Ski-Doos, and jeeps. I talked with a federal trapper. . . . He was making strych-nine baits. He told me that he was making two thousand, and had already made four thousand that had been distributed, and that he had put out forty stations of 1080 himself in the Meeker area . . . he is just one of eight or ten federal poi-soners in these two counties. . . . What has happened to majority rule? Who is to say that our fur-bearing animals are to be exterminated? Secretary Udall? Our Colorado district predator-control supervisor. . . ? A few greedy sheepmen? Doesn't any of the other citizens count? Is this poison program to be crammed down people's throats because of a very small minority? . . . There are some seventy thousand sheepmen in these United States . . . but there are millions of hunters, fishermen, and trappers who would vote out this predator control on the first ballot if it were brought to a vote. . . . I could go on for hours . . . on how the Fish and Wildlife Service handles their 1080 . . . how they just let the sheepmen come in and help themselves to the treated baits; and how they pass out strychnine pills by the box to sheepmen, and how the druggists . . . are all handling thallium poison and the sheepmen are buying it, and that's the worst poison known to man. It only kills six out of ten animals that get it. The rest go blind, their hair comes out, their toenails come out, or their teeth. And I could tell you how the sheepmen shoot game animals, deer and antelope, by the hundreds and treat them with poison on their own. I know where there is fourteen deer baits right now. . . . It would make your hair stand on end, all the things I really have seen."

Control, however, carried the day. Representative Dingell's bill to replace predator control with an advisory system died in committee. During the next three years, Dingell and other congressmen introduced similar bills, without results.

Recently, the executive director of Defenders of Wildlife, an indomitable woman named Mary Hazell Harris, who operates from a small office in Washington, was asked her view of the Bureau's reforms. She said that the Bureau seemed to be trying to make its program look better but that reports from her agents in the field indicated that the program was as "terrible" as ever. "They are still saturating the West with poison," she declared.

As an example of the Bureau's newest propaganda, she produced a poster that showed a clean-cut, smiling young employee of the Bureau against a background of birds and animals caught in the act of destroying property or endangering humans—a rabid fox biting a farmer, a starling eating fruit,

Young black-footed ferrets first venture out of the burrow at night. Later they appear in daylight and play like puppies. In autumn they disperse; each goes its solitary and mysterious way.

The plump, busy prairie dog (left) chooses the choicest grasses for its dinner. Prairie dogs are rodents related to squirrels but adapted to dig burrows. They are hosts of the black-footed ferret which lives in their burrows and preys on them for food. Without prairie dogs the ferret cannot survive as a species. Poisoning of prairie dogs has brought ferrets near extinction.

Prairie dogs must be wary for they are the prey not only of ferrets, but of coyotes, bobcats, hawks and owls. Their eyes are placed near the top of the skull the better to see danger coming from above. Their burrows are close together to form a "town." Group vigilance is their best defense. When a predator appears, lookouts give the alarm with a high warning "bark," and all citizens run for their holes. However this system is no defense against the black-footed ferret which creeps into their burrows at night and seizes them.

The black-footed ferret with its brilliant markings of black and shades of brown has the grace and beauty of a tiny tiger as it creeps through the grass of a prairie-dog town. No bigger than a mink, it depends on stealth, speed and courage to overcome its prey. Ferrets were probably never abundant even before man interfered with them. Because they were so rare and so elusive they were almost completely ignored by science. There are still many biological mysteries in their life cycle. For instance, what limits their numbers so that they do not overkill their prey?

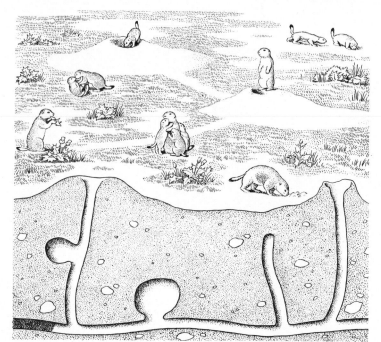

Prairie dogs' many activities are shown in drawing (left). One works on burrow while another does sentry duty. At top a trespasser is challenged. Others feed, groom each other and play. Labyrinthian burrows are connected underground. Prairie-dog social life is extremely elaborate. The population is divided into "coteries" whose members share their territory but repulse strangers from other coteries. Surplus prairie dogs form new coteries so population does not become too dense.

Bare mounds of earth around prairie-dog holes provide vantage point to watch for predators. Because of these mounds and because prairie dogs compete with cattle for grass they are hated by ranchers. Fifty years ago dog towns covered millions of acres, but thanks to relentless poison campaigns by state and federal authorities only a fraction remains. Since prairie-dog towns provide food and shelter for many other creatures, poisoning them is bound to have an effect on prairie ecology.

Sometimes a mother ferret will tour the prairie-dog town in daylight, disappearing underground as she inspects holes and popping out again. Ferret behavior is not yet understood.

These young ferrets, photographed at night, were discovered on a ranch near White River, South Dakota, an area where the only known remnant of ferrets survives. The Bureau of Sport Fisheries and Wildlife hopes to capture young ferrets and breed them as a hedge against extinction of the species in the wild, but in the past three years has not been able to find a litter to capture.

A remarkable series of pictures shows the mother ferret hunting to feed her litter. She crouches at a prairie-dog hole, enters it and moments later reappears carrying her victim. With some difficulty she drags the body through the grass to another hole where her young await her. These pictures were made at dawn after an all-night vigil. Observing and photographing ferrets is a difficult, often frustrating task that requires hundreds of hours. The elusiveness of the ferret is the trait most likely to cause its extinction. Since 1965 the Bureau of Sport Fisheries and Wildlife has tried to spare dog towns containing ferrets, but has been unable to devise any sure method of determining their presence. In the absence of proof that these *are* ferrets, the prairie dogs are poisoned.

A coyote "getter" (above) ejects cyanide into the mouth of any animal that tugs at its scented wick. It may kill many carnivores besides coyotes. In 1968 "getters" fired 200,000 cyanide shells and presumably killed that many animals. The Bureau also stakes out poisoned meat in chunks of fifty or a hundred pounds. The poison 1080 is so deadly that one bite (1.4 oz.) will kill a coyote. Other meat-eating birds and mammals are endangered. In 1969 the Bureau put out 11,423 bait stations of poisoned meat. No one knows how many creatures were killed. In some cases the corpses of victims are also poisonous, creating a chain of death.

DANGER!

Poisoned Coyote Bait in the Area!

OWNERS OF DOGS TAKE NOTICE

Poisoned meat baits have been staked out in the area to kill predatory animals which would harm your livestock and game animals. You are asked to stay away from them, and to keep your dogs away.

UNITED STATES DEPARTMENT OF THE INTERIOR
Fish and Wildlife Service
Bureau of Sport Fisheries and Wildlife

¡PELIGRO!

¡Carnadas Venenosas en Esta Localidad!

ATENCIÓN DUEÑOS DE PERROS

En esta localidad se han puesto carnadas venenosas para controlar animales silvestres de rapiña que matan el ganado y los animales de caza. Mantengan perros fuera de esta zona. No intervengan con las carnadas venenosas. Son peligrosos.

DEPARTAMENTO DEL INTERIOR DE LOS ESTADOS UNIDOS
Servicio de Pesquería y Animales Silvestres

COYOTE GETTER
EXPLOSIVE
DO NOT TOUCH

a bobcat killing a turkey, a coyote eating a lamb, and so on. The legend on the poster read, "Wildlife resources are of interest and value to all people of the United States. Basic policy is one of husbandry. Local population control is an essential part of management where a species is causing significant damage to resources and crops, or where human health and safety is endangered. Good conservation today—more sport tomorrow."

Miss Harris commented, "They seem to be taking advantage of the public's interest in conservation to fool people into thinking that somehow or other killing is conservation. They're just getting smarter and more pious."

In 1970, she continued, Representative Dingell had again introduced his bill. The future moves of Defenders of Wildlife were uncertain, Miss Harris said, but it was now considering filing a lawsuit against Wildlife Services.

Jack Berryman, who directs Wildlife Services from a suite of Washington offices decorated with photographs of animals and birds in blameless and appealing attitudes, is a stocky, gray-haired man with an open, vigorous manner. He sees himself as a professional conservationist and deeply resents the attacks of what he calls "the wild-eyed protectionists," who, he says, portray him and his field men as "blood-thirsty killers." When the attacks come from qualified scientists, he is even more indignant, and describes them as "little better than prostitutes."

The propaganda of Defenders of Wildlife, which frequently shows pictures of the last agonies of the animal victims of Wildlife Services, arouses just as much rage in him as Wildlife Services' propaganda against animals arouses in Miss Harris.

"Animal control is not an evil undertaking—it's amply

justified on the basis of economics, disease prevention, game protection, and other reasons," Berryman says.

He foresees that the nation's expanding population will require ever more killing of wild animals. His main concern, he says, is to have the killing done under professional direction, in order to minimize the needless sacrifice of wildlife.

If the conservationists begin a new attack, Berryman will be ready for them. He has prepared a voluminous record detailing reforms. It describes numerous meetings, training programs, and directives to re-educate the field men since he took over.

"It was not easy," Berryman says, "to change the thinking of men who for years had been praised for killing animals and suddenly were being vilified for it. Naturally they reacted defensively."

The Bureau's tables of animals killed show a reduction over the period 1965–68 of twenty-seven per cent in the number of bears, forty-six per cent in the number of bobcats, twenty-three per cent in the number of coyotes, and fifty-two per cent in the number of mountain lions. Berryman admits that such tables mean little, since they may reflect a change in the abundance of animals available to be taken, a change in killing technique so that bodies are not found, or a change in counting methods. For instance, coyote pups are now gassed in their dens, and are not counted. In some cases, the dose of poison is reduced, and animals therefore travel farther before they die. Nor do the new tables mention the smaller animals killed.

Understandably, Berryman is not keen on such tables, since they put ammunition in the hands of Miss Harris and her allies. In any case, he feels that a tally of lethal devices used is more significant. One of his charts shows that 1080 meat baits declined from 15,349 in 1960 to 11,423 in 1969, or about twenty-five per cent. Coyote "getters" are down thirty per cent from 1962 and traps down thirteen per cent. Strychnine baits, however, have risen about three per cent. Grain soaked in 1080 for rodents reached a high of 165,958 pounds in 1965 and declined to 126,552 pounds in 1968. The "man-years" of Wildlife Services employees have also declined slightly since 1965, but funds reached a new high of $7,300,050 in 1970, and Berryman foresees ever larger sums spent on control.

Berryman is confident that he can show that the Bureau is killing fewer animals over all but killing more where they "need to be killed." To him, the important factor is not the number killed but the economic assets protected. He also feels that he has had some success in persuading the sheepmen and others not to demand complete extermination of any animal.

Berryman dismisses as unanswerable the question of what constitutes "economic need" to kill animals—whether, for instance, the protection of ten sheep, a hundred sheep, or a thousand sheep justifies poisoning a given area.

"It is questionable whether local control can or should be the subject of economic analysis," he says. "To attempt such a justification could well be an exercise in futility."

Instead, he relies on drawing up a "work plan" in each state, and this is developed from the requests of the people managing the land, who presumably have some economic basis for their desire to have animals killed. While this procedure involves more formalities than the old PARC system, it is difficult for Miss Harris, for instance, to see it as a basic change, since both damage data and the definition of values are as hazy as before. Berryman's critics feel that he has merely shifted some of the onus of control from the Bureau to whatever agency asks for it.

The Bureau, Berryman admits, has taken no new steps to determine the total cost to the ecosystem of distributing lethal devices.

"There is not one ecosystem in the United States that is understood," he said recently. "If we waited until we understood an ecosystem, we would do nothing."

This determination to go ahead with a course while lacking data to predict its results makes some ecologists shudder. They view poison as a monkey wrench tossed into an incredibly intricate machine, and feel that it cannot be anything but detrimental to wildlife.

Berryman replies that scientists who "babble about the 'balance of nature'" are not taking into account how thoroughly that balance has already been altered, and must be altered in the future, for the "benefit of man." The new policies of the Bureau, Berryman believes, are best expressed in a policy statement issued in 1967. In this, for the first time, the government recognized the rights of what it calls the non-consumptive user of wildlife—meaning anyone, from bird-watcher to biologist, who values wildlife for a reason unrelated to sport or economics.

The statement said, "Conservation must be practiced . . . for the ever-increasing proportion of people who simply enjoy seeing and hearing wild animals in their native habitat. . . . The reduction or suppression of animal numbers should be undertaken only as a means of accomplishing specific management objectives. . . . Animal damage control . . . is defined as the management of damaging bird and mammal populations at levels consistent with the needs and activities of man."

People like Miss Harris are delighted to have their rights recognized, but they wonder whether "populations at levels consistent with the needs and activities of man" might not eventually mean levels of virtually zero. Berryman resents such suspicions and the general lack of gratitude and appreciation for the Bureau's achievements.

"The conservationists had better think twice before they try to abolish us," he says. "They might succeed. Then there would be no central supervision of control programs. The landowners would be left to their own devices. In my opinion, that would be ruinous to the nation's wildlife resources."

III

When Robert Henderson identified the black-footed ferret
on Earl Adrian's ranch in 1964, his first thought was that he
would love to study the species, but this was remote from
the job the state paid him to do—mainly, keeping track of
the populations of game birds and deer. His boss, Robert
Hodgins, the director of the the South Dakota Department of
Game, Fish, and Parks, like many game commissioners, is not
a scientist but essentially a politician. Hodgins was preoccupied
at that moment with a problem that had arisen when the
pheasant population in South Dakota declined sharply.

Pheasants are big business there. Hunting brings in twenty-
five million dollars a year. When pheasants declined, so did
revenues, and the Game, Fish, and Parks Department was on
the spot. Nobody knew why the pheasants had disappeared,
but most of the hunting clubs were convinced that foxes were
to blame.

Qualified biologists maintain that predators have little to
do with such population declines, and a study was then under
way at the South Dakota Cooperative Wildlife Research Unit
at South Dakota State University, in Brookings, to determine
just that point. Nevertheless, the state asked the Bureau to
assign extra men to kill foxes. The Bureau refused, pending the
outcome of the study, but Hodgins, acting on the recommendations of men in the Game, Fish, and Parks Commission
(the Department's parent agency), ordered an immediate war
on foxes. State game wardens roamed the countryside gassing

47

foxes out of their dens and clubbing them and their pups. The blitz destroyed sixty-seven hundred predators—most of them foxes, but included were coyotes, bobcats, and badgers—and also undermined the study. Relations between the Bureau and Hodgins were strained by the incident.

With pheasants, not ferrets, on his mind, Hodgins told Henderson he could do whatever he liked about the ferret as long as it didn't cost the state money or cause trouble. Henderson had also been in touch with Dr. Paul F. Springer, at the South Dakota Cooperative Wildlife Research Unit. Dr. Springer, a Bureau biologist, was the head of the Cooperative Unit, a laboratory that is supported partly by Bureau funds and partly by state and private funds.

He had been interested in ferrets for several years. The previous year, a mink rancher had donated a single male ferret to the university, but it died of pneumonia. Dr. Springer had wanted to make a field study of the species, and had discussed this with the local PARC man and in letters to Washington, but nothing came of his efforts, because there were no ferrets available for observation. Now, with a ferret available, Dr. Springer was determined to seize the opportunity.

The Bureau consented, and the study of the ferret became a formal Unit project. Its funds were modest; the Bureau contributed a thousand dollars, the National Park Service two thousand, and Dr. Cottam's Welder Wildlife Foundation five hundred. The next question was who should do the fieldwork, for neither Henderson nor Springer could leave his other work.

At this point, Earl Adrian stepped in. He said he wanted no "government people" on his ranch, but he suggested that his son, Dick, who had just graduated from Marquette University and was interested in wildlife management, might do the job. Henderson was asked by the Unit to help him. Accordingly, Dick was hired, and on August 17, 1964, he pitched a tent on his father's dog town and he and Henderson began their study, with Dr. Springer supervising from his post at Brookings.

The ferret had first been described by John James Audubon and John Bachman from a skin sent to them in 1851. They classified it as *Mustela nigripes*, or black-footed member of the mustelids, a large family that includes the weasel, the mink, the marten, the badger, the otter, and the skunk.

In fact, however, the black-footed ferret's closest relative is the European polecat which, when domesticated as a rat-catcher, is also called a ferret.

In 1896, when Dr. Clinton Hart Merriam, of the Biological Survey, tried to describe *Mustela nigripes*, he could find only half a dozen specimens in museums. In 1929, Ernest Thompson Seton, the naturalist, found records of sightings of *Mustela nigripes* to be so meager that he concluded the animal had always been rare and was probably waning. He predicted that the range of the ferret would turn out to be identical with that of the prairie dog, "unless we succeed in exterminating both species before sufficient notes can be made." He called the ferret "a robber baron securely established in the village of his helpless peasantry," noted that "its mating habits, call notes, love notes, song and amusements are wholly unknown," and went on to say, "We know that it . . . lives like a mouse in a cheese, for the hapless Prairie-dogs are its favorite food," concluding, "Now that the big Demon of Commerce has declared war on the Prairie-dog, that merry little simpleton of the Plains must go . . . and with the passing of the Prairie-dog, the Ferret, too, will pass."

For decades after Seton wrote, there was no real advance in knowledge of the ferret. Mammalogists continued to list it as a mysterious and, it was thought, increasingly rare species.

During the nineteen-forties, the lack of scientific knowledge about the ferret attracted the attention of biologists in the National Park Service. The problem was discussed by the executive committee of the American Committee for International Wild Life Protection in 1952, and Dr. Victor H. Cahalane, of the Park Service, undertook a field survey of the ferret's range. He asked the field men of the Park Service and the Bureau to report any ferrets they encountered in the course of their work. Cahalane collected reports of some sixty ferrets seen mostly during the period 1948 to 1952.

The sightings covered ten states, and stretched from northern Montana to New Mexico and Texas, but many were isolated instances. The only cluster of reports—sixteen of them—came from South Dakota, and Cahalane concluded that this must be the heart of the ferret's remaining territory. He noted that almost a third of the ferrets reported had been killed, and that most of the rest had been seen in dog towns slated for poisoning. While he was unable to prove that the ferrets would themselves be poisoned by feeding on poisoned prairie dogs or would starve when their normal food supply was destroyed, he believed that this was the most likely outcome. He urged further study of the ferret, and also suggested that some ferrets be trapped and released in protected prairie-dog towns in national parks.

The Bureau and the Park Service agreed with the latter proposal, but, except for one abortive attempt, did nothing about it. In 1953, Walt Disney was filming a movie called "The Vanishing Prairie," and a Bureau trapper caught five ferrets in South Dakota for Disney's use. One died in the trap; another died of a previous gunshot wound. The others survived the movie and were turned over to the superintendent of Wind Cave National Park in southwest South Dakota, where there were prairie-dog towns. Two escaped and the third was released, but no ferrets have been seen there since.

The Park Service biologist Walter Kittams is credited with keeping interest in the ferret alive during the next decade. He persuaded the Service to keep on trying to transplant ferrets to a safe spot, and got in touch with numbers of people, including Bureau trappers such as Pullins, who were most likely to see ferrets, and asked them to let him know of any sightings of ferrets, dead or alive. Henderson was one of the men Kittams had talked with about his interest, and from the start Henderson had responded warmly.

Henderson, a tall, jug-eared, intense man in his late thirties, combines the common western passion for the outdoors with an unusual reverence for it, perhaps shaped when he was a student at the University of Kansas, for one of his teachers there was Dr. Hall. Henderson has degrees in botany and zoology, and in 1961 he was hired as a game biologist by the South Dakota Department of Game, Fish, and Parks. The thought that he might be instrumental in saving an endangered species fired his idealism, and he included the search for ferrets in his fieldwork, travelling hundreds of miles over remote reaches of the prairie, scanning dog towns, and talking with ranchers and Indians who might remember having seen a ferret.

Kittams had compiled a list of past ferret sightings—the first step in an attempt to determine the status of a species—and Henderson began adding to it. The list was not heartening. In 1960, there were nine sightings (four of the ferrets were dead), in 1961 there were two, and in 1962 there were five.

In 1963, Henderson's wide search paid off, and he recorded sightings of eight live ferrets and four dead. But, in spite of countless hours of watching, it wasn't until he came to Adrian's ranch in 1964 that he saw a live ferret.

To an untrained visitor, a prairie-dog town is relatively featureless—an area of short grass or bare ground dotted with evenly scattered craters. The dogs are plump, tawny, short-legged rodents, weighing about two pounds. They are members of the squirrel family, and they have short, perky tails that jerk expressively. Like squirrels they sit on their haunches to observe what's going on. They are highly vocal, and signal to each other with a variety of calls. Their alarm call sounds vaguely like a bark; hence the name prairie dog. When an "all clear" is sounded after the departure of a predator, the whole town joins in a triumphal chorus.

The population of a town is divided into coteries of one or two males and several females and their young. Coterie members keep in constant friendly communication and guard their boundaries against trespass by non-members. This territoriality spreads the population and insures that the food supply is evenly distributed. Group vigilance protects the dogs against predators. Thus, the prairie dogs' social life is an important factor in their survival. It is also engaging to watch. The dogs' main business is feeding on vegetation and improving their labyrinthine burrows, but they interrupt it frequently to enjoy each other's company.

Whenever two prairie dogs meet, they greet each other with a kiss, touching their bared teeth together. Even in flight to a burrow, two passing prairie dogs pause for a hasty kiss. "At other times," Dr. John A. King, an animal behaviorist, has written, the kiss "is more leisurely and prolonged. Two animals will meet and kiss; then one will roll over on its back, still maintaining oral contact. Often the kiss ends with both animals rapturously stretched out side by side; they then rise and move off to feed with their bodies pressed together."

The kiss is probably a device to distinguish friend from foe. When two prairie dogs are uncertain of each other's identity, they creep toward each other on their bellies, flicking their tails and with teeth bared. If one is an interloper, he is intimidated and flees. If both are within their rightful territory, neither gives way, and they advance and kiss. After the kiss, they go on to what is obviously the pure pleasure of grooming. One prairie dog will nibble and paw the other, which will roll over on its back and respond with encouraging nuzzlings. All members groom each other regardless of sex or age, and this grooming takes up a good part of a prairie dog's day. The pups are especially greedy for it, chasing after the adults to attract their attention.

Prairie-dog pups emerge from their underground nurseries into what Dr. King calls a pup's paradise, in which they are gently taught the rules of behavior. All the adults in a coterie, male and female, kiss and groom any pup, and any coterie female will suckle him. His importunate demands for attention are borne with patience. When pups are small, they may wander into the territory of other coteries with impunity, but as they grow larger they are repulsed, at first gently, then more forcefully, until each pup learns the meaning of boundary and kinship.

Prairie-dog hostilities are mainly ceremonious. An invader is challenged to a form of combat that is emotionally satisfactory and remarkably harmless. It consists of threatening rushes, retreats, ritual sniffing and mild nips. Right determines might, and the contestant with the lesser claim to the territory soon retires.

From March until May, while females are busy bearing young, coterie rules are suspended. Yearlings and some adults then wander to the edge of the town, where they construct new burrows. Thus, the population is dispersed and the land not overgrazed, and in suitable habitats dog towns may grow to cover hundreds, or even thousands, of acres.

Prairie-dog towns play an important role in the lives of a host of animals besides the ferret. The dogs' activities have an effect on every form of life in the vicinity, including the insects in the soil beneath them, the vegetation around them, and the whole range of plains animals—reptiles, other rodents, birds, carnivores, and herbivores. Prairie dogs are selective feeders, choosing the plants that are most nutritive at a given time of year. They eliminate taller plants and encourage fast-growing weeds with abundant fruits and seeds, and the short blue grama, buffalo grass, and forbs.

As though to clear the town of cover in which predators could lurk, they clip non-food plants and leave them on the ground to wither. The ground in a dog town is usually barer than the surrounding area, and the variety of plants is quite different. Prairie dogs have an intimate relationship with grazing animals. The feeding of grazers, like that of prairie dogs, tends to spread blue grama, buffalo grass, and forbs. Early naturalists noted that prairie-dog towns followed the track of the buffalo. Buffalo moved constantly, seldom overgrazing, and so the prairie-dog population was large but stable. When cattle replaced buffalo, the cattle overgrazed, removing the tall grass, and prairie dogs increased far beyond their earlier numbers.

Not only do prairie dogs follow grazers but their towns are favorite gathering places for cows—or for buffalo, elk, or antelope, if they happen to be around. The trampling and manure of the cattle and the feeding of the prairie dogs make conspicuous changes in their little section of the world, but there are more subtle changes, too. Prairie-dog burrows are intricate catacombs averaging fifty feet in length. The distance between burrows varies, but the average number of burrows per acre is twenty-two. All this earth-moving changes the composition of the soil; the digging not only mixes the soil and aerates it but may enable it to hold water that would otherwise run off. The dogs further enrich the soil with the plants they carry underground, with their droppings, and with their bodies when they die. Thus, they help convert the prairie from silt to loam. The sites of abandoned towns turn green sooner in the spring than the surrounding land.

All in all, a prairie-dog town is something like a metropolitan center for other creatures. Ants, beetles, spiders, worms, and so on, come for the manure, for the seeds, or for each other. Horned larks, lark buntings, meadowlarks, plover, and mourning doves come for the insects and the seeds. Grouse perform their dances in the dusty earth. Prairie-dog burrows are cool in summer and warm in winter, and provide refuge for many uninvited guests. (One is the burrowing owl, which, like the ferret, is associated with prairie dogs and may be unable to carry on without them. The burrowing owl is now rare, and, because of the poisoning of prairie dogs, is likely to become rarer. Its extinction is quite possible.)

No one has ever calculated the effect on all these creatures when a prairie-dog town is suddenly poisoned with 1080 and "cleaned up" with cyanide cartridges thrown down the holes. The question is highly complex, and it is economically too unimportant to invite study, but within their microcosmic world the event must be a Hiroshima-like disaster.

The extent to which prairie dogs compete with beef cattle

55

for grass has never been scientifically determined, but the matter is more complicated than it seems. There are so many variables, such as the rainfall, the season, the choice of plants, and the condition of the range, that it is impossible to equate the foraging of a given number of prairie dogs with that of a given number of cows. Early cattlemen, however, merely looked at the barer earth around dog towns and concluded that their cattle were being robbed.

In 1902, Dr. Merriam, of the Biological Survey, computed by an unstated formula that two hundred and fifty-six prairie dogs consumed as much forage as one cow. This ratio has been quoted ever since as a definitive indictment of prairie dogs. In 1958, a study made by Carl B. Koford for the New York Zoological Society and the Conservation Foundation found this figure highly exaggerated and the results of applying any such formula misleading. "It seems that . . . there was a tendency among men of the Biological Survey to overemphasize rodent damage in order to gain support for the work . . . [of] predator and rodent control," Dr. Koford wrote.

One fact about prairie dogs is undisputed: they prosper and spread in conjunction with overgrazing, and thus may be blamed for a condition that was in fact brought on by the cattle. Poisoning prairie dogs will not restore overgrazed range unless the cattle are reduced as well. In the short run, prairie dogs may reduce the range capacity for cattle somewhat, but the full effect of their feeding is not understood. Koford found in almost every aspect of the prairie dogs' ecological role "an array of unknown relationships, conflicting data, and controversial ideas" that aroused misgivings about the ultimate wisdom of destroying them. The Bureau, however, does not share his doubts.

Seton put the range of the black-tailed prairie dog during the latter part of the last century at about six hundred thousand square miles—an area that may have held as many as five billion animals. Cattlemen began poisoning the dogs around 1880. In the early nineteen-hundreds, state governments joined the war on prairie dogs, and the Biological Survey began poisoning dog towns on public lands. About 1916, the war intensified, and spread to cover millions of acres. In the thirties, the Civilian Conservation Corps and the Works Progress Administration helped with the job. In the forties, 1080 came into use, and the prairie-dog population shrank rapidly. Prairie dogs now cover only a small fraction of the area they inhabited fifty years ago. The Bureau still carries on the war against them, poisoning over a quarter of a million acres a year.

Small colonies of prairie dogs are being preserved in national parks and by some landowners, and so, because the species recovers rapidly, it will probably not become extinct. But as a common animal of the Great Plains the prairie dog has all but disappeared.

Until quite recently, the single area of the plains that had escaped the full brunt of poisoning was South Dakota. This was partly because much of it was Indian land, and so inspired less federal zeal for improvement, and partly because for some years it was on the fringe of PARC's operations. In 1964, South Dakota had the greatest remaining population of black-tailed prairie dogs. The heaviest concentration was in five counties in the south-central part of the state. It is here that most of the ferrets reported in the last six years have been seen.

To study the ferret on Earl Adrian's ranch, Henderson and Dick Adrian watched the south dog town around the clock, by day with binoculars and at night with a powerful spotlight (which did not unduly disturb the ferret). They were delighted to find that the ferret was a female with a litter of three, and were also pleased to rediscover the second family. Black-footed ferrets, Henderson found, are extremely beautiful little animals. They are small—no bigger than a mink. Their round heads, large round ears that stand out alertly, inquisitive shoe-button eyes surrounded by the mask of black fur, and black noses give them a face that is utterly beguiling. Their long, tubular bodies are pale brown on the back, shading to buff and almost white underneath. Their legs are black to the shoulder, and the ends of their tails are black, too. They look like the prettiest of stuffed toys.

The study lasted from August 1964, through August 1965, and made it abundantly clear why so little has been recorded about ferrets. They are among the most elusive of animals and the most difficult to observe. Most of the day, they stay belowground, although an adult may bask for a time in the sun or make brief trips around the prairie-dog town. At night, the mother ferret, who rears her young without help from the male, emerges for longer hunting forays and glides quickly from burrow to burrow, sometimes entering and shortly popping out again, at other times staying down for a longer time.

In early summer, the young do not appear at all, but when they are half-grown the mother begins to bring them out at night. At first, the young are timid, and the mother must coax them out, or sometimes drag them out by the nape. Later, they gain confidence and follow her in response to a low, plaintive call note. Eventually, Henderson observed, she would lead her young about the town in single file, so that they resembled a small toy train. As the young ferrets lost their fear of the open, they began to play, leaping and tussling like puppies. By mid-July, they were partly weaned. Several times, Henderson saw the mother come out of a hole with a dead prairie dog in her jaws and drag it to the burrow containing her young. On another occasion, she cached dead prairie dogs in a burrow one night and led the young to it the following night.

In early August the young sometimes came out in daylight, playing near the burrow entrance, and at night began to hunt on their own. By the end of August, they were full-grown and independent. Dr. Springer believes that the young probably travel in search of new dog towns, but almost nothing is known about their dispersal. When they leave, they are vulnerable to predators, and if dog towns are far apart they must support themselves on other prey. If they scatter too widely, they may be unable to find mates. Thus, even if a ferret family escapes poisoning, the destruction of dog towns may have an equally lethal, though slower, effect on the species.

One thing that Henderson and Dr. Springer wanted to learn was how ferrets could be discovered. Ferret tracks are visible only in mud or snow or freshly dug earth, and the animals rarely leave droppings aboveground. One of the few clues to a ferret's presence is the behavior of the prairie dogs, which often fill the burrow it occupies with soil, apparently trying to entomb it. This presents no problem to the ferret, which digs itself out when it chooses and then disinters its young, but a number of stopped-up entrances are a hint that a ferret is about.

Ferrets also do a lot of digging in prairie-dog burrows; no one is sure why. When excavating, the ferret backs out of the hole holding dirt against its chest with its front paws. As it drags the dirt away from the hole, kicking it backward, it leaves a trench in the loose earth. The trench is a sure sign of ferrets, but its absence is not proof that no ferret is there, for the industrious prairie dogs often destroy it.

Although the ferrets live in the midst of their food supply, they apparently must struggle for their meals. Henderson and Adrian noticed that as the summer progressed the female ferret became thin and unkempt from her labors to feed her young. Prairie dogs weigh as much as ferrets and are not quite pushovers. Henderson saw dogs chase the mother ferret, and even tussle with it. Ferrets probably hunt mostly at night, creeping through the long tunnels and seizing prairie dogs asleep in their chamber. How many prairie dogs a ferret requires is not known, but there seem to be biological factors that keep the ferret population in balance with its food supply so that the species does not eat itself out of house and home.

IV

The discovery of the black-footed ferret in South Dakota came just as the Leopold Report was being studied and before Gottschalk and Berryman had taken over at the Bureau. The policy of protecting endangered species had been announced only very recently, and Dr. Springer's study of the ferret aroused little interest in Washington. Around this time, Springer learned that PARC was planning a large campaign of prairie-dog poisoning in South Dakota the following summer. The Bureau's South Dakota office had made an agreement with the Bureau of Indian Affairs to poison the Pine Ridge Indian Reservation, which held the highest population of prairie dogs in the state and was probably the last stronghold of the ferret. Springer was concerned about the effect this program might have on ferrets. He discussed it with the regional supervisor, Clarence Faulkner, who instructed the district agent that poisoning at Pine Ridge should be done with "consideration" for any ferrets that might be present, and that if any were found Springer was to be consulted before poisoning proceeded.

The reservation, the home of the Oglala Sioux, is a tract of a million and a half acres of grazing land—ninety miles long and fifty miles wide—west of the town of White River. It was once twice as large, but over the years white ranchers gained title to half the Indians' land. Even what remains is not truly in the hands of the Sioux. Forty per cent is leased to white ranchers—a situation that has come about largely because the Indians, lacking capital to buy cattle and seldom able to get loans from banks controlled by white ranchers, have been forced to lease the land. Grazing policies, such as the number of cattle per acre, annual rents, and prairie-dog poisoning, are in the hands of the Bureau of Indian Affairs.

Pine Ridge escaped massive poisoning until the nineteen-fifties. About eighty thousand acres were treated then, but by 1964 the prairie dogs were again widespread. The ranchers holding leases complained to the B.I.A. that prairie dogs were reducing their income, and, on the recommendation of the B.I.A.'s range managers, the Sioux Tribal Council agreed to the poisoning, some of the cost of which would come out of tribal funds. The B.I.A.'s Land Operations officer, Duane Moxon, made arrangements with Jim Lee, the district agent for PARC, for the poisoning to be started in the summer of 1965.

Henderson had not been able to search the reservation thoroughly for ferrets, but he had collected quite a few reports of sightings from the area. He and Dr. Springer were convinced that a high proportion of whatever ferrets remained on earth were directly in the poisoners' path. In April, they met with Moxon, Lee, and Faulkner to see what could be done to protect the ferrets.

The B.I.A. and PARC men were reluctant to make any concessions. They conceded that the Bureau of Sport Fisheries and Wildlife's new policy was to protect any endangered species, but they challenged Springer to prove that prairie-dog poisoning would harm the ferret population. They questioned the assumption that ferrets depended on prairie dogs for survival, and expressed doubt that ferrets would eat poisoned prairie dogs and die from secondary poisoning. Since no specific studies had been made, Springer was, of course, helpless to demonstrate anything conclusive. The best he could arrange was an agreement that Henderson and Adrian would be allowed to search dog towns ahead of the poisoning crews. If they found a ferret, the area would be temporarily bypassed.

After the meeting, Springer wrote to Gottschalk to express misgivings. He pointed out that, of a total of ninety ferret sightings over the years in South Dakota, about a third were on or close to the reservation. He also wrote that, on the basis of all existing evidence, he thought it highly likely that the ferret did depend on prairie dogs and would eat poisoned prairie dogs and succumb to secondary poisoning.

He particularly questioned the poisoning of a tract of land forty miles long and twelve miles wide just north of the reservation. The War Department had purchased most of this land—348,000 acres—from the Indian and white owners in 1942 for use as a bomb range, and now it held twenty thousand acres of prairie dogs, probably the highest concentration in South Dakota. The range supported some ten thousand cattle owned by Indians and absentee ranchers. These leases were of no benefit to the Sioux, because the range was federal land, and the annual income from it, which amounted to $161,604, went into the United States Treasury. Nevertheless, the B.I.A. was asking PARC to poison the bomb range for the benefit of the leaseholders.

Springer reminded Gottschalk that it is always difficult for the Bureau to acquire habitats for wildlife, and noted that it didn't seem logical to destroy an ideal ferret habitat already in federal hands. He argued that PARC, instead of

63

asking him to prove that poisoning would harm ferrets, should be asked to prove that poisoning was harmless to them. Gottschalk apparently was not impressed, and the bomb range remained in the plans for poisoning Pine Ridge.

The whole ferret matter might have ended there had not Dr. Stanley Cain, Assistant Secretary of the Interior for Fish and Wildlife and Parks, who had jurisdiction over the Bureau, received a call from Dr. Cottam, his former colleague on the Leopold Board and something of an elder statesman of conservation, who had heard that the Bureau was about to further endanger an endangered species. Dr. Cain was distressed, and just a few days before the poisoning was scheduled to begin he called Gottschalk, Berryman, and officials of the Bureau of Indian Affairs and the Park Service to his office to discuss the question.

The Bureau of Indian Affairs, responsible not to Dr. Cain but to the Assistant Secretary of the Interior for Public Land Management, protested that to halt the poisoning program would victimize the Indians for the sake of an unimportant and possibly nonexistent animal. Dr. Cain asked Gottschalk and Berryman for information on the ferret, and he was told that they possessed very little. They pointed out that contracts for the poisoning work had been signed, that Indian crews had been hired, and that the 1080 to do the job was already in the warehouse at Pine Ridge. Implicit in the situation was the fear that if the Bureau withdrew from the program it would jeopardize relations with its "sister agency" the Bureau of Indian Affairs, and possibly cause a commotion at a higher level. Furthermore, if the Bureau of Indian Affairs chose to go ahead and use the poison anyway, Dr. Cain could stop it only by an appeal to Secretary Udall, who had not been informed of the ferret's plight. Dr. Cain thus found himself helpless to stop the momentum of the system.

Finally, the officials devised a compromise that, it was hoped, would allow the Bureau to safeguard the ferret and still poison the prairie dogs. The scheme was embodied in a policy statement, which conceded that "any form of control directed to the prairie dog will inevitably have some influence upon the ferret," and described the dilemma: "The Department has the responsibility for protecting rare and endangered species and also to control animals significantly detrimental to the best interests of man."

The solution was less forthright. It made equal promises to both sides: "It shall be the policy of this Department to initiate an intensive survey of the black-footed ferret to determine precisely those areas where the ferret must be protected and the best methods for assuring its protection. Control bait will be made available by the Bureau . . . for prairie-dog suppression as soon as [it has] investigated any area proposed to be treated and . . . determined that it is not occupied by the black-footed ferret."

Just how the Bureau was going to determine the absence of ferrets was left happily unspecified. Perhaps no one had thought about it too deeply. The Bureau issued a news release confidently announcing "a program to protect the endangered black-footed ferret and to control its more numerous associate and prey, the prairie dog." Since the Bureau itself had said that "any form of control directed to the prairie dog will inevitably have some influence on the ferret," the announcement had a rather dreamlike quality of paradox.

The responsibility for carrying out this program fell to Berryman, and he hastily ordered the poisoning held up until a way to make "ferret surveys" could be devised. The reaction in South Dakota was mixed. Henderson and Springer were elated. Moxon, the B.I.A. man, was annoyed. Jim Lee, the PARC man, who had worked closely with Moxon, was also less than enthusiastic. He found sympathy among friends in the state Game, Fish, and Parks Department, where he had a close relationship with Director Hodgins' second-in-command. The state was not directly involved with the Pine Ridge problem, since it had no jurisdiction over Indian or federal land, but Dr. Cain's policy statement applied equally to private land, and Hodgins decided that this was an invasion of states' rights.

"For many years, the black-footed ferret has been protected in South Dakota under State Authority," he protested in a letter to Gottschalk. "By what authority does a Federal agency assume management of any resident species?"

The Pine Ridge Tribal Council, for its part, was dismayed to learn that an animal it had hardly been aware of was going to cost it money. The Bureau of Sport Fisheries and Wildlife had decided that the Sioux should pay part of the cost of the ferret surveys. Thus, from the start Berryman found the Bureau of Indian Affairs, the state, the field men of the Bureau of Sport Fisheries and Wildlife, and the Indians arrayed to resist the policy of protecting the ferret.

Berryman dispatched regional supervisors from Minneapolis and a man from Washington to South Dakota to see what could be done to straighten things out. The start of the poisoning program was postponed for three weeks, and in this period there was a round of discussions on how best to carry out the awkward assignment. The delay displeased the Bureau of Indian Affairs. Gottschalk assured them that it was temporary. Then, firmly gripping both horns of the dilemma, he sent word to the regional office that the Bureau of Sport Fisheries and Wildlife "attached great importance" to safeguarding the ferret and that it was essential to get on with prairie-dog control as quickly as possible.

The task confronting the field men—determining whether ferrets were or were not present in each dog town before deciding whether to poison it—must have struck them as absurdly difficult. Observations by Henderson and Adrian had indicated that ferrets show themselves only briefly in daylight. If the general location of a ferret was known, the field men might be able to sight the animal at night by catching its green eyeshine in the beam of a searchlight, but to cover thousands of acres with a searchlight would be clearly impossible.

The only clues to the presence of a ferret—trenchlike diggings and plugged prairie-dog holes—were slim and short-lived. Finding ferrets was clearly a job that required infinite time and patience—elements that were in short supply just then. To judge by the ferret studies made before then, one man watching a hundred acres of prairie dogs for three days had at best a slim chance of seeing a ferret—provided that one was present. At this rate, a man might cover a thousand acres in thirty days, and it would take ten men a month to cover the ten thousand acres scheduled for poisoning. Even then, failure to see a ferret would not prove that no ferret was present.

Eventually, Berryman decided that two extra men would be hired to make the surveys. They were to take their orders from Lee, but Dr. Springer was to set standards for their work. From the outset, this forced marriage between research and control was none too happy. Dr. Springer's authority was limited, and Lee did not welcome any interference with the control program. Henderson was particularly unpopular with Lee, because his opposition to poisoning was well known, and so, although he had more field experience with ferrets than anyone else in the world, he had no official place on the team. Springer announced, however, that he wanted Henderson's help, so Henderson was grudgingly included.

Shortly thereafter, Springer, whose base at Brookings was several hundred miles from Pine Ridge, asked Henderson and Dick Adrian to meet with Moxon and Lee to iron out the final details of the surveys. At this meeting Henderson found, besides Moxon and Lee, three men from the B.I.A. and three control men. The meeting was hardly harmonious. Moxon challenged Henderson's right to take any part in the arrangements, and Henderson replied that he was both Springer's deputy and a representative of the state. Since the state had shown little sympathy for the ferret, it was obvious that this was shaky backing.

Lee, in charge of the meeting, introduced two old-time trappers named Burgee and Barnes as the "ferret experts" hired to make the surveys. In Henderson's view, their attitude was no different from that of any of the Bureau's other "gopher chokers." Both men had seen ferrets from time to time in their years of poisoning prairie dogs, and Barnes had trapped the ferrets Walt Disney used in "The Vanishing Prairie." In a rough way, they might be called "naturalists," but their orientation was an odd one for the task at hand.

Henderson asked Barnes how he planned to search for ferrets. Barnes declined to specify, but in answer to another question he said he had two cages in which to trap and hold ferrets. Adrian asked Barnes what he intended to feed captured ferrets. Barnes said he wasn't going to feed them anything. Lee remarked that the ferret program was greatly overrated. In his opinion, he said, it would be better to poison the prairie dogs first and do the research later. Henderson said that the research should be done first, since the reservation might be the last place in the United States where ferrets could be saved.

Laughter erupted around the table. When it died down, Moxon announced that he had detected what he called "a public-relations problem" with the Indians, arising from having too many people looking for ferrets. It had been decided, he said, that Henderson, Springer, and Dick Adrian would be barred from the reservation. Lee nodded agreement. He said that matters relating to Indians had to be handled carefully, and that since the ferret surveys were his responsibility, he felt any search by Henderson, Springer, or Adrian to be unnecessary. There the meeting ended.

The episode was smoothly translated into official language by Moxon. He informed his Washington superiors that "in the interest of public relations and expediency" he had decided that ferret surveys would be conducted "only by procedure established" and "other activities discontinued as unnecessary and detrimental to the . . . protection of the black-footed ferrets. We feel very fortunate to have Mr. Burgee and Mr. Barnes with their extensive experience in observing and handling black-footed ferrets, conducting the survey."

Gottschalk and Berryman, eager to avoid further friction with the B.I.A., decided to appoint a young biologist named Lorin Ward to supervise Burgee and Barnes and a third trapper in Springer's stead. In mid-August, Ward and the three trappers set forth, driving and walking over the endless, empty grasslands day after day, scanning the dusty mounds of the dog towns with binoculars and checking some of the holes for signs of ferrets. Behind them were the poison crews, bags of poisoned oats slung over their shoulders, who dropped a few grains at each hole. At one small dog town, what might have been ferret droppings were found, and the town was bypassed. Otherwise, the search was uneventful. When it ended, six weeks later, 12,350 acres had been certified "clear" of ferrets and 8,500 acres poisoned.

Ward reported to Washington, "We can't say there are no ferrets in this area. All we *are* able to conclude is that we did not find . . . positive signs of their presence."

Outside the reservation, Bureau trappers were instructed to look for ferrets before poisoning. None were found, and 2,634 acres of land were also poisoned. The Bureau's efforts on behalf of the ferret that summer had cost an extra $17,000.

PARC's old enemy Defenders of Wildlife shortly got wind of the procedures followed in South Dakota and published a furious article, "How to Endanger a Ferret," in its magazine, *News,* questioning the good faith of the Bureau's survey effort and charging that Dr. Cain's policy had been emasculated in the field.

Gottschalk and Berryman were angry and hurt over what they felt was an unjust attack. They believed that they had made unprecedented efforts, braved the wrath of the B.I.A. and Hodgins, and, by devising the surveys, taken the only means open to them to help the ferret. In their view, they deserved bouquets from conservationists rather than the same old abuse. Gottschalk answered a questioning taxpayer by saying, "This was one of the most closely supervised control operations ever undertaken and is a credit to those responsible for its conduct. . . ." He didn't mention that since no ferrets had been found, none had been protected.

After being ousted from Pine Ridge, Springer had to confine his ferret work to studying data collected by Dick Adrian, who was spending a second summer watching the ferrets on his father's ranch, and by Henderson, who was still collecting reports of sightings. Dick Adrian decided at the end of the summer that he had seen enough, and he quit the project. His place as researcher for the Unit's ferret study was taken by Conrad Hillman, a young man who was brought up on a farm in North Dakota. Hillman had just graduated from Utah State University with a degree in wildlife management, and was making the ferret study the subject of his Master's thesis. He felt, as Henderson did, that the ferret must be saved, and the two worked closely together.

After the first summer's search, Gottschalk and Berryman were aware that the ferret question was by no means resolved. Pine Ridge had been only partly poisoned, and the rest of the job would take two more summers, at least. There would also continue to be requests for the Bureau's services on private land within possible ferret range. The ferret problem would be with them as long as there was evidence that any ferrets survived.

The obvious solution—to stop poisoning for several years, until the ferret had been fully studied and a captive breeding population safely established—was out of the question, they felt. Politically, this course had little to recommend it. The ferret was an obscure cause, unlikely to generate much public interest. The Bureau was estranged from organized conservationists as a result of past hostilities. Nor could the conservation forces be any match for those interested in control. Ever since the Leopold Board's report came out, the livestock industry and its supporters in Congress had been watching the Bureau suspiciously, ready to fight any reduction of control. Berryman had been trying to reassure them that what he called "the new look in predator control" would be as effective as the old. If the Bureau stopped control to spare the ferret, the livestock men would conclude that it was knuckling under to conservationists. They would view the precedent of valuing wildlife above dollars as dangerous indeed, and their alarm would make it even more difficult for the Bureau to reduce its poison programs.

Then, there was the matter of what would happen in the field if the Bureau refused to poison ferret areas. The B.I.A. and the landowners could poison prairie dogs on their own, with any of a number of available poisons and without even the slight protection that the surveys had afforded the ferret. Only the Secretary of the Interior could halt poisoning by the B.I.A., and only an act of the state legislature could halt private landowners. Neither action was likely.

Gottschalk evidently decided that his best course, therefore, was to go on with control and to continue to believe that surveys protected ferrets. He wrote indignantly to the National Audubon Society, "I would like to state emphatically that no control measures are undertaken until we are convinced that an area containing prairie dogs has no ferrets. That statement deserves to be reiterated: *no control except on ferret-free areas.*" How he arrived at such a conviction would be hard to explain.

Gottschalk was well aware that in the annals of conservation the ferret was an important test case. If the ferret vanished, conservationists and scientists would blame the Bureau. In devising means to avoid poisoning the ferret—

other than prohibiting all poisoning—the Bureau was badly handicapped by ignorance. It would have been very helpful, for instance, to know how many ferrets existed, and where, and whether their situation was as critical as it seemed. Were ferrets scattered over a large range, or were those in South Dakota the last of their race? How many prairie dogs were required to support a ferret family, and how thinly could the ferret population be scattered and still survive? Most helpful of all would have been to find a way to locate ferrets without endless and costly hours of search. The ferret's elusiveness, which had served it well in a wild world, was now the trait most likely to hasten its destruction.

In the hope of answering some of these questions, the Bureau assigned a biologist to work full time on the ferret project. He was a young man named Donald Fortenbery, who had previously worked in predator control and might be presumed to understand both sides of the problem. In January 1966, Fortenbery moved into an office in Rapid City, and Henderson and Springer turned over to him much of their data and took him to the Adrian ranch, where Fortenbery soon saw his first ferret. Fortenbery's job, however, was not only to study individual ferrets but to try to define the ferret's original range and its present one, to estimate the number of ferrets surviving, and to discover how ferrets are affected by such variables as food, climate, and "land-use practices"—among them poisoning.

His studies were to be tactfully separate from the activities at Pine Ridge, where Lee continued to have charge of the surveys. "Your role will be to make an occasional field appraisal of the techniques being used, to satisfy yourself as to their adequacy commensurate with the scope of the problem," Fortenbery was told by the Bureau's Washington office. "You should not expend your time in routine participation in the pre-control survey exercise." Fortenbery went to work in his office, assembling data on file cards, plotting lines on maps and graphs, and racking his brain for a way to determine the presence of ferrets.

In July 1966, Hillman found a female ferret with five young on a ranch west of White River. By great good fortune, the rancher, a young man named Jim Carr, possessed a strong interest in wildlife and an aversion to poisoning. He was pleased and proud to harbor ferrets, and eager to have them studied. Hillman pitched his tent on Carr's dog town and spent the summer watching the ferret family.

At about the same time, Fortenbery learned that the Defense Department had declared the bomb range surplus land. He explored the range and found it to be a dramatically desolate piece of landscape with a minimum of good grazing land. Although two-thirds of the dog towns had been poisoned in 1965, he still felt it would be ideal for a wildlife refuge, and particularly for a ferret and prairie-dog refuge. In a report to Washington, he described it as an "area [of] pinnacled spires high and somber, stark buttes topped with western juniper or buffalo grass, by flat tables two to three hundred feet high with precipitous sides . . . low sandhills, and high prairies . . . tortuously twisting intermittent streams which have carved rugged, deep, steep-sided canyons . . . springs . . . yield good water and marshes [suitable for waterfowl]."

Although it was ideal for a varied animal population, wildlife was not abundant, perhaps because of hunting by Indians and poachers, perhaps because of the 1080 bait stations that the Bureau had put there to guard a small flock of sheep owned by one of the most influential woolgrowers in the state. Neither coyote poison nor hunting had bothered the prairie dogs, and they had thrived there until the poison crews had arrived the previous year.

"They are very efficient at their job," Fortenbery wrote of the poisoners. "I spent one day looking at practically every town that had been poisoned . . . and saw less than twenty-five dogs. By late fall the same story can be told for the rest of the area. The Bureau of Indian Affairs is . . . pushing the poisoning program which Wildlife Services is carrying out. . . . I don't disagree basically with prairie-dog control. . . . I question poisoning prairie dogs on . . . government land for the questionable benefit of eight or ten ranchers; particularly in view of the fact that a great part of this area will probably be given to the Badlands National Monument, who will then spend public money trying to restore the prairie dog. Dogs haven't been poisoned in this area since before World War II. Why then shouldn't poisoning wait until the disposition of the area has been decided? One or two or even three years more of living with dogs is not going to force the ranchers out of business. I believe that with the land situation in the U.S. what it is we can ill afford to tie up a quarter of a million acres for the personal benefit and satisfaction of eight or ten ranchers. Here, in South Dakota, at least, is probably the last place where one can see real concentrations of prairie dogs. I have no personal knowledge that ferrets actually exist on the range, but they have been reported there. . . . I can think of no reason why they shouldn't be there, and there is every reason why they should. I suggest that we . . . try to get a moratorium on the range until the General Services Administration disposes [of it]. . . . I further suggest that we bid for a portion of this area for a ferret project. . . .

75

It would seem that if we are going to try to protect the ferret . . . then the wisest course is certainly not to destroy the dogs on one of the last areas where they exist in any numbers and where their conflict with man is at a minimum."

A ferret refuge had a great deal to commend it. It would be a buffer between the Bureau's conflicting responsibilities. If ferrets were safely preserved in a refuge, the question of whether they were being poisoned elsewhere would be less crucial. Best of all, the ferret might thus be saved. Accordingly, the Bureau dispatched a representative to a hearing before the House Committee on Interior and Insular Affairs, which was considering the disposition of the range.

Representative Berry, of South Dakota, still an ardent enemy of non-marketable wildlife, ridiculed the Bureau. He said it was difficult for him to understand why a Bureau that had been poisoning ferrets and prairie dogs for thirty years was now trying to save them. The room rocked with laughter. "I was not asked to testify," the unhappy Bureau man reported later. "In view of what appeared to be a hostile reception . . . it would probably have served to inflame an already unreceptive audience."

The Bureau narrowed down its request to an area of twenty thousand acres in the northeastern part of the range which had not yet been poisoned, and presented the case for the ferret to the General Services Administration. The Bureau underscored the point that Gottschalk had refused to concede to Springer the year before. "The area lies in the heart of the range of the . . . ferret. . . . It goes without saying that it is necessary to preserve the prairie dog in order to preserve the ferret," it said.

Pending the outcome of its effort, the Bureau ordered

76

poisoning halted on the bomb range. The B.I.A. immediately rose to protest this "unilateral action," and the Bureau hastily explained that it intended to exempt from poisoning only the twenty thousand acres that it hoped to obtain, and forty-two thousand acres adjoining it that the Air Force hoped to retain. Then it resumed the "cleanup" and poisoning of the very area it had itself called "the heart of the range of the *endangered* black-footed ferret."

For the second summer, ferret "surveys" were conducted. Two Bureau trappers, under Lee's direction, looked for ferrets on land scheduled for poisoning. They turned up not a single sign of a ferret. Teams of poisoners moved across the reservation, and some eight thousand acres of prairie-dog towns were destroyed.

On October 15, 1966, the cause of the ferret and its companions on the road to extinction won a victory in Congress with the passage of the Endangered Species Act. This legislation declared that the loss of native species of wildlife was unfortunate; directed the Secretaries of the Interior, Agriculture, and Defense to protect threatened species and preserve their habitats insofar as this was "practicable"; and directed the Secretary of the Interior to prepare a list of such species as an official guide.

The first list contained the names of thirty-six birds, six reptiles and amphibians, twenty-two fishes, and fourteen mammals. The mammal in perhaps the most precarious position was *Mustela nigripes*. Along with this paper victory went an appropriation to the Bureau research center at Patuxent, Maryland. There the Bureau hoped to establish a stock of captured ferrets. But even such an apparently innocent project as breeding ferrets ran into complications. Hodgins, who was then engaged in negotiating a new agreement with the Bureau, refused to allow the capture of a "resident species." It was not until late 1969, when a new state-federal treaty had been signed, then he gave his consent.

Meanwhile, Dr. Ray C. Erickson, the assistant director for Endangered Wildlife Research, began preparing for the arrival of ferrets at Patuxent by building pens and breeding domestic European ferrets as a pilot project. These experiments have gone smoothly, and Dr. Erickson foresees no great difficulty in raising captive black-footed ferrets provided enough breeding stock can be procured. To have a large enough gene pool, it would be necessary to start with three litters—about a dozen animals. Since ferrets are presumed to be polygamous, Dr. Erickson hopes he will have more females than males. After two generations, if all goes well, there should be enough young to start releasing them in protected dog towns in parks and refuges.

Dr. Erickson's hopes of capturing ferrets were raised when, in the summer of 1969, a graduate student working with the Cooperative Wildlife Research Unit located a litter on land that the rancher planned to poison. The rancher was persuaded to refrain from poisoning, and Dr. Erickson made plans to capture its next litter the following summer. Unfortunately, in 1970, this ferret apparently had no young. Only one other ferret was located that summer. In September, Fortenbery sighted one on a ranch thirty miles south and east of White River, but by then the young ferrets, if there were any, had dispersed. Thus Dr. Erickson's breeding project had to be postponed to yet another year. For the time being Dr. Erickson has ruled out capturing any ferrets on the Carr ranch, deeming them safer and more useful in the wild where they provide the only known breeding stock that is not in danger of poisoning. Even here problems arose when the ranch recently changed hands. Whereas Mr. Carr had highly prized his ferrets and felt that the grass lost to prairie dogs was negligible, the new owner, a man named Edward Nielson, was less sympathetic. The Bureau found it necessary to pay him $2 an acre—a total of $600 a year—as reimbursement for grass lost through sparing the dog towns. This is a rather high rent for housing a few ferrets and may prove a burden the Bureau will not carry indefinitely. On the other hand it may be that it is only through arrangements such as this, paid for either by public funds or conceivably by private conservationists, that prairie dogs, and thus ferrets, can survive.

Fortenbery, meanwhile, continues to collect reports of ferrets from people here and there—park rangers, ranchers, Bureau trappers. In 1970, in addition to the two ferrets sighted near White River, there were reports he considered credible from Utah and Kansas and one from Wind Cave National Park in western South Dakota that seemed possible.

Despite his diligent assembling of records, Fortenbery's chart of the ferret's range is based on too little data to be really enlightening. He has no idea of the rate at which the ferret has diminished; all that is fairly clear is that it *has* diminished. There is a sprinkling of reports of ferrets from states other than South Dakota, but Fortenbery is unsure if they indicate only scattered individuals or if undiscovered pockets of ferret population exist here and there outside South Dakota.

He believes the answer may depend on the history of poisoning, but, again, records are scanty. He also thinks that a full-scale effort—perhaps twenty men working for a period of two or three years—could find whatever ferrets exist in

South Dakota, but there is no prospect of such an undertaking. Though he has tinkered with camera devices and lures, he has been unable to devise any way to find ferrets other than by an exhaustive search. Fortenbery concedes that surveys such as the Bureau conducts are unlikely to find ferrets except by a stray bit of luck, but he feels that they are worth conducting on that chance. Of one thing he is convinced—that for any population of ferrets to survive there must be prairie dogs.

In the summer of 1968, Congress divided the South Dakota bomb range among the rival claimants—the Sioux tribe, the Badlands National Monument, and the range's former private owners. Roughly half the range goes to the Badlands. The decision to keep or eliminate prairie dogs there will be up to the Park Service. On the rest of the range, the owners will be free to destroy all surviving prairie dogs. Although the Bureau did not get a ferret refuge, it is not entirely displeased with the outcome. It has negotiated an agreement that will enable it to protect prairie dogs (and ferrets) on the forty-two thousand acres that the Defense Department is keeping. Fortenbery estimates that there are thirty dog towns, totalling three thousand acres, on this land, and a ferret was seen there by a Bureau biologist on September 26, 1968.

Thus, the Bureau continues on its schizophrenic course—its left hand struggling to preserve the ferrets while its right goes on destroying their habitats. Officially, the Bureau still professes to believe that it is not endangering ferrets, on the ground that its surveys prove they don't exist in the areas to be poisoned, and it still leans heavily on ignorance of the biology of the ferret, contending that there is as yet no proof that poisoning prairie dogs damages the ferret population.

"We are still not sure that the conflict between poisoning and the ferret is clear-cut," a spokesman said recently.

Conservationists doubt both propositions, but for obvious reasons have not been able to produce a poisoned ferret. Without a corpus delicti, there is no case. The Bureau's own policy on control, adopted in 1967, states that when such precautions as surveys are inadequate to protect a threatened species, no poisoning will be undertaken. As long as surveys find no ferrets, the Bureau can poison prairie dogs and remain snugly within this policy.

Ironically, it was only when a ferret actually turned up that the fallibility of the survey system was demonstrated. On September 2, 1969, a trapper who had nearly completed the job of poisoning a dog town north of Pine Ridge happened to see a ferret, and poisoning stopped. On three subsequent nights, Fortenbery searched for the ferret but didn't find it. In this instance, the pre-control survey had been inadequate, and the Bureau had indeed violated its own policy by poisoning in the vicinity of a ferret. The episode brought no change in an otherwise smoothly working system, and the fate of the ferret is unknown.

When the survey system was so hastily devised back in 1965, it may have seemed a credible solution of a problem, but it has been of more service to the Bureau than to the ferrets. From the point of view of the ferret, it has changed nothing. Every acre that was scheduled to be poisoned has been poisoned, and each year new poison programs to kill prairie dogs will be deemed necessary. At the same time, the Bureau assures the public that it "exempts from control" dog towns inhabited by ferrets. The future of the ferret now rests on the outcome of the race between the Bureau's left hand and its right. If Dr. Erickson can capture ferrets, and if his breeding project succeeds, it is possible that the species will remain on earth. Meanwhile, the Bureau is not likely to swerve from its grim business. The cause of the ferret was never a match for the forces working against it. It is not remarkable that the ferret and its supporters lost. What is remarkable is that there was even a small struggle.

A while ago, I went to South Dakota to visit the scene of the ferrets' last stand. The grasslands were a pale yellow green, the winding valleys and watercourses darker with the shade of thick shrub and small trees. Rocky hillsides were dotted with evergreens. Along miles of straight, empty highways, crossroads were far apart, houses were rare, even cattle were few. Everywhere, the land stretching to the horizon seemed prosperous and undisturbed, offering everything needed to sustain countless forms of animal life. There were water, sun, flowers, grass, seeds and berries, the shelter of shrubbery and canyons, rock ledges and buttes, even high crags for eagles and hawks.

There are indeed a great many animals there—deer, coyotes, bobcats, badgers, rabbits, and small rodents. Perhaps as many animals survive there as anywhere else in the United States. They are important to the human population. Killing them provides almost every man and boy in the region with his greatest source of excitement and entertainment. Almost every driver of a pickup truck has a gun with him, in case an animal is seen on the road. Hunters rent small planes from which to shoot coyotes and bobcats. The bounty plus the price of the pelt pays the cost of the plane. Jeeps make it possible to explore the trackless grasslands for birds, deer, or whatever else turns up.

In some circles, a popular sport is running coyotes with

packs of dogs, which tear the quarry to pieces. Target shooters spend their Saturday mornings on prairie-dog towns picking off the small, upright figures of the prairie dogs. Even schoolchildren are enlisted. A group called Pheasants Unlimited offers prizes to the children who kill the most predators for "conservation." In addition to the hundred and thirty-one thousand dollars South Dakotans pay the Bureau to eliminate predators, the South Dakota Department of Game, Fish, and Parks has wardens who are also engaged part of the time in killing wildlife. The Department pays hunters eighty-seven thousand dollars a year in bounties.

F. Robert Henderson had left South Dakota in June 1968, sad and bitter that his efforts on behalf of the ferret had come to naught. Dr. Springer had been transferred to less controversial research in North Dakota. Jim Lee had also departed, and the new state supervisor for Wildlife Services was Wesley Jones, a dry New Englander in his mid-forties, who expressed no doubts about the wisdom of killing animals that cause economic damage. He also expressed considerable anatagonism toward "protectionists" who represent this work in ugly terms. Asked if he thought any species should be exterminated, he reflected for a few moments and said that except for the rat "they all have some redeeming features, I guess."

For Jones, the ferret situation has been a ticklish problem—one that complicates the work of control and has considerable potentiality for causing trouble. His attitude toward protecting the ferret was cool but correct. His concern, he said, was to see that the trappers followed the procedures ordered by Washington. Of the animal itself, he said, "It hasn't been proved to me that the ferret *is* endangered. If it is, I don't know whether it is worth saving at financial sacrifice to a landowner. I think those who benefit from something should pay for it." He was unconvinced that poisoning endangers ferrets, he said.

Bill Pullins, a big, strong man in work clothes, with faded reddish hair and a wind-burned face, was angry and puzzled over the whole matter. "It sure has made more goddam trouble," he said. "I wish I'd never said nothing about it. I don't see all this fuss over ferrets. Outside of saying, 'We got 'em,' what's the sense? The damn protectionists try to make it look like people working for the government are doing a mean, wrong job. It ain't fair. Nobody kicks when a sportsman kills a coyote. If the protectionists had coyotes and coons eating up their property, they'd damn well want to get rid of them."

Jones had as his assistant a slightly built young South Dakota native in his late twenties named Leonard McDaniel, and it was his job to pick up reports from and transmit orders to ten Bureau trappers and one pilot west of the Missouri River. I found McDaniel's air of western manliness even more conspicuous than that of most men in the area, and much of his small talk hinged on hunting experiences—shooting a badger's head off at four feet, or picking a bobcat off at a hundred and fifty yards. He was also a mine of anecdotes illustrating the high cost of animal damage—foxes that chewed the tails off cows, coons that laid waste acres of corn, and so forth. He began working for PARC in 1962, to pay his way through college, and has had little use for "protectionists" ever since he found his classmates whispering that he was a "poisoner."

McDaniel drove me across the plains in a shiny new government station wagon to meet a crew that would be poisoning prairie dogs on a ranch on Pine Ridge. We turned off the highway onto a rutted single-track dirt road that wound between soft, grass-covered hills. Clumps of small sunflowers and spiky purple blooms bordered the road. It crossed a canyon flanked by turreted sandstone formations and came to a windmill, where water spilled from a tank. A few cattle drinking there were watched over by the rancher, an old man on a black cow pony. He was Edison Larvie, and he told me that he had been ranching there fifty-two years and owned a thousand acres.

"It's a nice place, if you don't mind the rattlers and the thunderstorms," he said.

On a nearby pasture was a hundred-acre dog town. He had decided to have it poisoned because badgers sometimes dug out the holes and a horse might break a leg if it stepped in one. "We call 'em widowmakers," he said, smiling.

I asked Larvie if he had heard about the ferret.

"Yes, I have," Larvie said. "Just heard the government is checking on 'em. I guess these little critters is danged hard to see."

I asked if he would be willing to protect one if it were found.

"Sure thing," Larvie replied warmly. "I heard these things is getting scarce."

A pickup truck piled with sacks was parked on a slope below the windmill, and three Indian men in bluejeans, cowboy hats, and checked shirts were sitting by it. With them was a burly young man named Dick Lemm, a student at Black Hills State College, in Spearfish, who had been hired for the summer to continue the Bureau's ferret surveys. Lemm said that he had already checked the town over and that the crew was ready to begin poisoning.

The men poured grain from the sacks into bags, slung

these over their shoulders, and moved into the meadow. Small earthen craters were scattered over the hillside, and here and there prairie dogs could be seen running through the grass to their holes. Their warning calls sounded from all sides as the men approached. An owl rose, battling the wind. Lemm and McDaniel walked through the nodding heads of grass, ankle-high and dotted with blue flowers. The sky was beautifully clear, the sun benevolent and warm. The wind pressed the grass into silver waves ahead of the work crew, who were now walking from crater to crater on a methodical course, dropping poisoned oats from long-handled spoons as though they were leaving a tiny gift on each doorstep. The prairie dogs had disappeared.

"They don't come out and eat right away," McDaniel said. "But if you come back later and watch, you'll see 'em feeding. Then, all of a sudden, you'll hear that little ol' dog scream, and see him head for his hole."

ILLUSTRATION CREDITS

Defenders of Wildlife, page 12 (all photos).

F. Robert Henderson, page 1 (both photos); page 8 (both photos).

Bill Ratcliffe, courtesy of The National Audubon Society, page 9.

B. J. Rose, page 10 (both photos); page 11 (all photos).

Leonard Lee Rue III, page 2; page 5; page 6 (both photos); page 7.

Scientific American, page 4 (top photo).

Glenn Titus, page 3.

U. S. Department of the Interior—Fish and Wildlife Service, page 4 (bottom photo).